THE QUEEN'S COUSIN

Raymond Wemmlinger

SAPERE BOOKS

THE QUEEN'S COUSIN

Published by Sapere Books.

24 Trafalgar Road, Ilkley, LS29 8HH

saperebooks.com

Copyright © Raymond Wemmlinger, 2025

Raymond Wemmlinger has asserted his right to be identified as the author of this work.
All rights reserved.

No part of this publication may be reproduced, stored in any retrieval system, or transmitted, in any form, or by any means, electronic, mechanical, photocopying, recording, or otherwise, without the prior written permission of the publishers.
This book is a work of fiction. Names, characters, businesses, organisations, places and events, other than those clearly in the public domain, are either the product of the author's imagination, or are used fictitiously.
Any resemblances to actual persons, living or dead, events or locales are purely coincidental.

ISBN: 978-0-85495-675-3

1

1594

The hoped-for words burst from the midwife: "A boy!"

The sweet music of his first wail sounded, followed by an eruption of jubilant cries from the courtiers crowded into the bedroom. In the birthing chair I threw back my head triumphantly. The rich drapes and hangings of the room seemed to swirl in a riotous celebration of exploding colours.

Waves of voices, frenzied with excitement, washed over me as the midwife's attendant swiftly detached the cord.

"The year 1594 is blessed!"

"A prince of Scotland!"

"A king to follow his father! God willing, on the throne of England also, a king of all Great Britain!"

Triumph again surged through me, vanquishing the pain and exhaustion of my labour. I looked up into the beaming face of the midwife, holding the child. "Give me my son!" I cried, with a loudness that silenced the room. Two of my women, the young ones who'd come with me from Denmark, rushed in beside me, one of them pulling down my soiled dress and the other wiping the dampness from my forehead, and smoothing back my hair.

The midwife gently handed me the child, still naked, and I cradled him in my arms, pressing him against me. The women fell back, the crowd of faces across from me becoming clear, some of the highest-ranking earls and countesses of Scotland. Shortly after midnight they had begun to gather, and over the past two hours as many as possible had pushed into the room, waiting silently, or speaking in hushed tones. It was time to acknowledge them, and I addressed them in a firm voice, in perfect English, not forgetting in my moment of glory to keep it free of the accent I had worked so hard to overcome: "I have done my duty, and given this kingdom an heir! I present you with your prince, descended from the kings of Scotland, and England, and Denmark. Go, one of you, and tell the king he has a son."

The child's breath was steady against my hand, and I marvelled that he felt no less a part of me than he had during the months within, growing, making ready for his entrance into the world. Beside me, one of the women fell to her knees and rested her head against me: it was Anna, from Denmark, at twenty, barely a year older than me, and with whom I shared a name. Since coming to Scotland, though, except for my formal signature, I'd chosen to be called Anne. It had been the name of the mother of the English queen, Elizabeth, and although that Anne hadn't fared so well, her daughter had reigned successfully for nearly forty years. Elizabeth, now old and with no child to succeed her, had no closer relative than her cousin King James of Scotland. And King James now had a son.

A cup of wine was presented near to my lips, the herbs in it pungently bitter, but I shook my head. Why should I need it now, when I hadn't before? The pain hadn't been as bad as I'd been led to believe, just different, unusual. Certainly not enough for me to scream, as I'd been encouraged to. But I'd already decided that was something I would not do, not in front of the courtiers, or my gentlewomen. They would never hear me scream, or cry out. No queen should be heard doing that.

The castle bells began ringing exuberantly, announcing the birth. Within minutes the more distant ones in Stirling below the castle would sound, and by morning others would ring all over Scotland. In the bedroom the courtiers were talking excitedly, some of them pressing forward for a closer look at the prince. But they still held back, waiting until the king had seen his son.

I felt a slight cramping. I'd been told to expect the afterbirth, and the midwife, observant and skilled, said at once, "Good, it comes quickly." She squatted again before me, the women closing in around her. "Take the child," someone said, but I held him tightly. I drew a deep breath, exhaled and felt another passage — smoother, with no pain.

And then it was done. "Such an easy labour," the midwife said. "As though he just slid out!"

One of the women came forward with soft linen, but I refused it. "No swaddling yet, not until the king has seen him. Seen every part of him!"

I looked down at my child. He wasn't crying, and his eyes were open as he squirmed gently in my arms. I rested one hand on top of him, covering him with my spreading fingers, a gesture of protection, but not against the cold. Although it was February, the bedroom was perfectly comfortable, the winter winds reaching Stirling Castle on its perch above the open and rolling landscape dispelled not only by the strength of the walls, but also by the fire roaring in the huge fireplace beside me.

A gentleman stepped out of the crowd. "The king is on his way, Your Grace," he said as he bowed, and then retreated.

Suddenly I didn't want James to see me in my dishevelled state. "Quickly, help me into the bed!" I ordered.

The women stared at each other, and one began to protest, but the midwife said, "She is strong, this one. Do as she says."

Already I was standing, holding my child, and Anna and another woman grasped my elbows and guided me to the bed. The crowd in the room hushed, entertained by the spectacle. The deep blue velvet covers were pulled back and the women helped settle me into a seated position, propped up on the pillows. Another woman brought a light wrap and tucked it around my shoulders, and I was pleased it was white silk. White was my favourite colour and suited me best, against my white complexion, my blue eyes and pale-yellow hair. I'd been blessed with Danish beauty — my hair was thick and curly and held styling, and I was slender but well-shaped, and not overly tall, which was undesirable in a woman. James admired my beauty, and I wanted no detraction, no image of dishevelment seeded within his thoughts.

"Make way for the king!" boomed a voice from the other side of the room. The crowd parted and James appeared, everyone bowing and curtseying smoothly as he strode past. His gangly and uneven gait sometimes gave him the look of a man much younger than his twenty-eight years, but today it conveyed only excitement. And for once his usually sad-looking face, with his hooded and pensive dark blue eyes, and slightly downturned mouth, looked happy.

"Anne!" he called, even before he'd broken away from the courtiers. Although he always appeared to deftly ignore their presence, he never showed any emotion towards me around them, a sign that in truth his indifference to the court was studied and practised. But today, upon reaching the bed, he dropped to his knees and buried his face in my shoulder, close to our son. His yellow hair, darker than mine but just as full, brushed against my face. Although he was hatless, he still wore a cloak, heavy and fur-lined, and boots instead of slippers, telling me he'd been outside. Always restless, always moving,

James often paced in the paved court of the castle when circumstances prevented him from riding, a favourite pastime, the speed of the horses allowing him to throw off agitations or tensions. During the last month of my confinement, confined to the bedroom, I'd sometimes thought how unbearable being so contained would have been for him.

Across from us, rapt silence prevailed, the courtiers transfixed by the display of regal love and affection. James lifted his head and looked down at the child for a long moment. Then he stood, took him from my arms, and brought him to the foot of the bed, where he held him up for the court to see.

"Henry Frederick Stuart!" he declared, his voice loud and firm. "Prince of Scotland. Henry for my father, Henry Stuart, Lord Darnley, as well as the great Tudor King Henry the Eighth, the father of my most esteemed cousin Queen Elizabeth, and his father King Henry the Seventh, from whom she and I both descend. And Frederick, from King Frederick the Second of Denmark and Norway, father of my most beloved queen."

As though in reply, or perhaps in response to the loudness of his father's voice, the child let out a small cry. Delighted, the court broke into applause. "Long live Prince Henry Frederick!" some called out, and the others followed, causing the child's crying to continue. Then, James came back to my side. But instead of returning the child to me, he turned to my women. "Where is the nurse?" he asked quietly.

From behind them a young woman stepped forward; she too had recently given birth and would amply provide for another babe. I'd wanted one woman to serve as daily and wet nurse.

James handed the child to her, then turned back to the court. "The queen needs to rest," he said with authority. "Go to bed, all of you." Dismissed, they in unison bowed and curtsied, and backed out of the room.

The quiet following their departure was soothing. James threw off his cloak, which Anna caught before it reached the floor. He then told her to bring him paper and pen. To me, he said, "I will write to your mother and tell her you are safely delivered of the prince. Also, a note to your brother, to go with the council's formal announcement." I smiled, but was now finally starting to feel drained, and even a few simple words of thanks required too much effort. It was as though, now that he was present, the responsibility of strength could be shifted to him. But I was glad he had chosen to stay in my room to attend to the letters. He enjoyed being near me, the result of his isolated and lonely childhood, and we'd been nearly inseparable since our marriage. I had once asked how he had sufficient time to attend to his kingdom while spending so much with me, but his bemused reply had been that his talents were such that it took him but a fraction of the usual time it took other men to accomplish what needed to be done.

He began pacing back and forth before the fireplace, measuring and calculating his words. The note to my brother — who'd succeeded my father as Danish king — required especially careful wording, as a communication from king to king. James's use of language, whether written or spoken, was always adroit and shrewd. It was one of the reasons my English had quickly become so good.

Anna returned with the paper and pen and ink. As James sat down at the table on the other side of the fireplace, she came and arranged my pillows more comfortably. I was about to tell her to have the nurse bring Henry to me when they'd finished swaddling him, but was just then overcome by a powerful need to sleep. Everything was fine, and in order, and the security I felt in James's presence allowed me to relax. The child was in good hands, and could do without me for a little while.

When I awoke, it was morning. The heavy drapes had been removed from the windows and the bedroom was full of light. James was still there, but the table had been removed and replaced by the cradle we'd had readied. For once, he was still as he sat beside it, gazing down into it. His long smooth face, not handsome, but interesting, usually showed little of what he felt. But today his fixed expression was one of resolve, determination, and pride.

He noticed I was awake. "I had the curtains removed," he said. "Perhaps you'd have slept more had I not."

"It was enough."

He looked back to the cradle. "Your women protested. They said it was usual for the room to remain dim for some time to remind the newborn of the womb. But this is not a usual child. I wanted him greeted by the light of the rising sun. Nothing less is right for him."

I sat up. It felt as though I'd slept for days, instead of a few hours. Suddenly, concern gripped me. "Did he feed?"

"As though famished. He took to the nurse immediately. The midwife says she's never seen so robust an infant."

"You decided his name."

We had discussed the name Henry, but the addition of Frederick had been a surprise. "It pleases you?" he asked.

"Very much." The choice had been appropriately respectful of me, the daughter of one king and sister of another. Often, I hadn't felt James's equal, considering his great learning and political sophistication, achieved by necessity from his earliest childhood to survive the bitter power struggles of Scotland. But my having produced a male heir seemed to have adjusted all inequity. I was now the mother of a prince, who would in time replace his father as king, just as my brother had replaced my father. An emptiness within me had been filled, and as I sat in my great bed of state surrounded by soft pillows and luxurious covers, for the first time I truly felt his equal. The triumphant feeling of my first moment after delivery soared within me once again. "It was right to include the second name," I said with confidence. "Henry Frederick! He will be a great king one day."

James said nothing, but half-turned towards me.

"You sent the letters?" I asked.

"Yes. One to Elizabeth, also."

"A wise decision." Although it was irritating to have to treat the English queen with such deference, we were both in agreement it was of paramount importance for us to try our utmost to gain the English throne. Elizabeth would not name a successor, and there were other candidates, but lately she had shown signs of favouring James's claim. The English political landscape was perilous, fraught with the same religious divisions as in Scotland, but with much higher stakes because of the great wealth of England. There had been quiet messages from leading nobles there that James would likely be most acceptable to the many factions. But it was the queen who would have the final say as to who would succeed her.

James turned away from the cradle and came to me. His face as he drew closer was startling, with an old man's expression I'd never seen before. There was a grim set to his mouth, and for once his heavy-lidded eyes looked wide and alert. The change was so pronounced that for an instant it seemed he wasn't the same person. But his uneven gait was reassuringly familiar, and his lanky figure, in dark green doublet and hose, was a little dishevelled, because his fine clothing never mattered to him.

He sat down on the bed beside me, and the strange look vanished; it was him again. He leaned in and lightly brushed his lips against mine. Then he sat back, gazed at me fondly, and asked, "You are well?"

"Yes. It was no ordeal, just an exertion. God willing, I will pass through it again."

He took one of my hands in his. The touch was sensuous and conveyed desire, although his face showed nothing of it, which was how it always was with him. His desire for me was strong; there were never any tales of mistresses. "Many times," he murmured.

Then he stood up and went back to the cradle. Looking down into it, he said, "It was right for Henry to be born here at Stirling."

I had at first planned to be confined at Holyrood Palace in Edinburgh, which felt appropriate as Scotland's capital. But James had then subtly indicated that he felt Stirling to be more suitable, so at the last moment I'd changed my plans. We were almost always in accord with one other, and when not, it was with the merest effort that we became so. Stirling was the most modern of Scotland's royal castles, having been renovated by James's grandfather into a modern palace to rival those of Europe, especially the great French chateaus. Within the medieval fortress had been constructed a palace of beautifully decorated rooms. It was a fitting setting to receive a new prince, and I'd assumed that had been the reason for the choice.

"I was thinking about that while you slept," James said. "Most of my childhood was spent here."

The remark was odd, since what he'd told me of his orphaned childhood hadn't been happy. He'd been raised by strict and austere Calvinists, who had come to dominate Scotland, despite the continuing presence of Catholics. Although I conformed, I'd been raised Lutheran in Denmark, closer to the old Catholic way. Privately, I felt there were aspects of all three faiths that were admirable, especially the beauty of the Catholic art, condemned by the Calvinists as idolatry. James, despite his Calvinism, had years ago grasped the importance of careful diplomacy in navigating such difficult religious waters; from time to time he commented that all Scots were his subjects, no matter their faith. It was that particular trait which appeared to recommend him to the English as the king to follow their ageing queen in a country divided among Anglicans, following the church as reformed by King Henry VIII; Puritans, who took those reforms much further; and the traditional Catholics.

The religious tensions, and their extreme expressions, had underscored James's childhood, and it surprised me that he would view it with nostalgia. I was about to say so, but before I could, he said, "And it was here that my parents fell in love."

I stared at him in surprise. He almost never spoke of his parents. Before his first birthday, his father had been murdered, and it was generally believed that his mother had been responsible for it. Shortly afterward, the Scottish lords had revolted against her and she had fled to England, where she had been held in captivity for the next eighteen years, during which time she had continuously plotted against the English queen. Finally, seven years ago, Mary, Queen of Scots had been executed.

James continued, "My mother had lived here too as a child, before she was sent to France." His tone was empty, as though he was thinking aloud. "Likely in these very rooms." He looked around, deliberating. "Where else would it have been? These are the queen's rooms, not the king's."

There might have been a touch of the look of the strange old man again, but if so, it was gone in an instant. He exhaled deeply and ran a hand through his hair, turning to me. "I will leave you now to the care of your women. Today, a new world opens for us. I have much to do."

As I watched him leave, an inexplicable feeling of fear rose in me. I called out, "James!"

He turned and looked back at me, his face questioning. But I had nothing to say. He half smiled at me. And then he left.

Immediately, Anna and the other women entered from the other side of the room, where they had been waiting for James to leave. The women went to the baby, while Anna came to me.

But my unsettled thoughts were still about James. "He did turn back," I said, more to myself than Anna.

She looked at me with concern, her blue eyes narrowing. "Sad thoughts on such a happy day?" she asked in terse English. Long ago we'd made a rule never to speak Danish to each other, except if there was a need for secrecy. Her English was as perfect as mine.

"The king was strange … different. He even looked a little different to me. He spoke of his childhood. And his parents."

She didn't reply at once, but her lips pressed together as she thought. As a child, Anna had wanted to become a nun, either Catholic or Lutheran. Her father, a court official in Copenhagen, had been appalled and had flatly forbidden it, instead placing his beautiful daughter in my mother's household. There, she had become my friend. But she had never overcome her distaste for court life, which her keen observations had only increased.

"The Queen of Scots is dead," she said flatly. "The English queen tried for years to avoid executing her, but her tricks caught up with her and made it necessary. The king understood this. He barely protested when she died. He wants the English throne."

"So do I," I said vehemently. "It is his birthright; his claim is the senior one. And now it is my son's birthright as well!"

"Forget Mary of Scotland."

"I nearly had, but then he spoke of her today."

Anna frowned. "With sympathy? That would be strange. I am told he was taught to hate her, as the murderess of his father."

"No, not sympathetically, but not with hostility, either. It was as though he'd never thought much of her before. Or his father. He said they'd fallen in love here at Stirling. Strange to think that a marriage that ended with such hatred might have started with love."

Anna scowled distastefully. "Oh, what of love? The only love that is true is the love of God. Other love isn't for me. Work is for me. Helping others. Helping you." She folded her hands in front of her. "Forget your husband's rambling thoughts of the past. They were provoked by the birth of the child, and will soon fade. Your fears come from disruption of your body's humours from the birth. Soon you will be yourself again."

The memory of James's look of determination as he'd stared down at our son, and that strange, unfamiliar expression that had come over him, still disturbed me. I certainly hoped that Anna was right.

"Forget the Queen of Scots," she repeated. "Think of the English queen, and what is to be gained for your family. Think of the brilliance of what your future can be, and not of the tragedies of the past."

She snapped her fingers twice behind her, drawing the attention of the women cooing over the cradle. One of them reached in and gently lifted up little Henry, and brought him to me. As I took him in my arms, I felt a powerful sense of fulfilment. This tiny creature would grow into a great and powerful king, and make more of an impression on the world than I ever would. But until then it would be my place to watch over him, protect him, and guide him. And as I held him tightly, and he looked up at me, I felt as though I could never let him go again.

2

Over the next months we stayed at Stirling, rather than change through the seasons among our various castles as had been our custom. The smaller room off my bedroom was turned into a nursery, and Henry thrived there as winter melted into spring, and then summer. He was a robust and handsome baby, seldom crying and easily soothed when he did, although seeming very serious. I remembered the infancies of my younger brothers, and by comparison Henry didn't smile nearly as much. But when he did, after exertions on my part to coax one from him, I felt like I had been gifted with a priceless jewel. I also came to treasure being the first one he would lay eyes on when he awoke. Every morning I would go to his cradle, the women and nurses falling back so that only I stood beside him, and I would wait for his eyes to open. The look of recognition when he woke, secure and serene, brought me great joy. *I am the mother of a prince*, I would think. *I will be remembered as the mother of a great king.* And on the days when I was rewarded with one of his rare smiles, my happiness would last for hours.

James, too, was thrilled with his new son and visited him daily, but more formally, in the middle of the day, accompanied by several of his gentlemen and councillors. His engagement with Henry was more reserved than mine, which was to be expected, given James's temperament. He rarely held him. But there was a quiet intensity to their meetings. I tried to be present for them, sometimes actually holding Henry, and when I wasn't, I had the attendant nurses describe them to me afterward. When I asked if the baby had smiled at his father, the answer was always no. Yet it was still evident, to me as much as the other women, that the two were deeply bonded, almost as though Henry had been born with an understanding that the responsibilities of his father would someday be his.

James had resumed his nightly visits to me as soon as was acceptable, a month after the birth. I welcomed him back into my bed, and he would stay the night, the bed curtains drawn tightly around us for privacy while my women slept on their pallets as far away as possible on the other side of the room. But in the mornings, he never accompanied me to see Henry wake, and when I returned to my bed he was always gone.

A magnificent baptismal celebration was planned for August, at which Henry would formally be given the titles Duke of Rothesay, and Prince and Great Steward of Scotland. When the time arrived, it was almost as though Henry understood its significance, for he stood alone for the first time just a few days before. No one, though, had really been surprised by the earliness of this milestone, for Henry had previously sat up alone at midsummer. The speed of his progress had filled me with pride, for it heralded a child full of eagerness to grow and take his place in the world. Yet at the same time I had felt a little sadness at the retreat of the tiny baby I'd held in my arms. His sitting up and then standing alone took him further from the time he had been a part of me.

Among the crowd of delighted women encircling Henry as he'd stood beaming with pride at his accomplishment, only Anna had noticed the shift in my mood. She had then whispered in my ear to remember the loss of Mary, the mother of Jesus. Anna had always been attracted to the old Catholic ways, and perhaps had even converted. Although she didn't hide her interest from me, she knew enough not to let me know if she had. Religion in Europe had political dangers attached to it, and those in power understood it was best to keep certain things to themselves. But she also knew that since the birth of Henry I'd begun to find the Catholic veneration of Mary intriguing. "As a story," I'd prudently remarked to her after discussing it.

There had been no question that Queen Elizabeth would be Henry's godmother, and the day before the baptism her representative ambassador arrived at Stirling with his entourage. We received him in the large Inner Hall of James's apartments, both dressed in garments of the finest cloth of silver, and seated side by side beneath the numerous carved oak heads of historical and mythical figures fitted into the coffered ceiling. I disliked the room because of the heads, finding their unrelenting stares disturbing, but they served as an appropriate statement of royalty and splendour. Everything possible would be done during the ambassador's stay to show him and his attendants that Scotland wasn't a primitive backwater, but modern and sophisticated, if still a bit unruly, and that James would be well experienced to manage the affairs of England when the time came.

The earl Elizabeth had chosen as her emissary was noticeably young, barely out of his teens — a quiet statement that despite her advanced age, she was thinking of the future of her kingdom as she looked toward Scotland and celebrated the birth of a prince. After bowing low to us while extending the formal greeting of Elizabeth, he asked to see Henry, who was brought in from where we'd had him waiting, just out of sight, fully expecting that the earl might ask for him. Anna carried him to the earl, who bowed low once again.

"Set him down," James said quietly, causing the earl to look up at him questioningly. But when Henry stood firmly on his own feet before him, he smiled broadly and bowed again, and offered him greetings from his cousin Elizabeth. Behind the earl, the other gentlemen of the English party all murmured with approval. Most were young also, young enough to someday become the subjects of the child before them.

The audience concluded, and James was already standing, ready to accompany the earl to a meeting with the Privy Council, when he turned to me. "Anne," he said, as I too stood. "At the ceremony tomorrow, the Dowager Countess of Mar will carry Henry from his nursery to your presence, before the court."

The news was surprising, and unwelcome. "There is no need for it," I objected. "I am his mother. It is fitting for me to carry him in."

"I wish to honour her, for the long service her family have shown me."

Up above, the carved heads seemed to be scrutinising me, waiting for my response. I hesitated; I wanted to do it myself. But many members of the court stood close to us, along with the English earl, listening to the exchange. It wouldn't do to disagree in front of them, but I didn't want to give up my place to her. I was about to protest again, when James, still looking at me without expression, said evenly, "It is done, Anne. The countess arrives later today. Please see that she is welcomed. Considering her advanced age, she honours us as well." And then he turned away with the earl, followed by both of their gentlemen.

With effort, I remained composed. The decision stung even more because he'd informed me of it in a manner calculated to allow me no room to argue or even discuss it. James had never treated me so before, which made it worse. I smiled, trying to conceal my anger in front of the gentlewomen walking beside me and trailing behind on the way back to my apartments.

Once there, after Henry was settled back in his cradle and being gently rocked by the women whose job it was to do so, I beckoned for Anna to follow me to my outer bedroom, away from the others.

Before I could speak, she asked, "Who is this Countess of Mar? Has she ever been at court?"

"No. She was the king's childhood governess; she and her husband had charge of him here at Stirling. Her son, now the earl, isn't much older than him, and they became great friends. They still hunt together today. He is Governor of Stirling Castle, although he hasn't been here at all since we arrived. I've met him, but not her. But if she's anything like her son, she'll be a very prim and proper Calvinist."

The silver coronet I was wearing, one of several I used for minor state occasions, suddenly felt uncomfortably tight, and I pulled it off, freeing my compressed hair. I shook my head, feeling the hair brush against the upright ruffled collar, spread wide behind my neck. "I don't like that the king did this without consulting me." My fingers wrapped tightly around the coronet. "I am the queen, and Henry's mother!"

"Perhaps there wasn't time to tell you," Anna said prudently. "It diminishes you not at all, madam."

Soothing words were never her way, but her simple statements often had that effect. I could easily be making too much of it. There was no reason for me to begrudge an old woman a place of honour.

"Yes, the king has been busy with the baptism preparations," I agreed. I handed her the coronet. "Put that away. Tell the women I want to go to the garden." I felt tense and agitated, and the best way for me to throw it off was to go outdoors. My bedroom, with its heavy brocaded draperies and richly coloured curtains, wall hangings and carpets, which usually felt so welcoming, suddenly seemed oppressive, while the elegantly repeating gold patterns in the dark green coffers of my own ceiling looked a tangled and confusing mess.

Outside, the sky was a solid blue with only the wispiest of clouds. At Stirling the sky dominated the landscape, even on overcast or rainy days, but especially when the weather was clear. The garden beneath the windows of my suite was low, with flower beds but no shrubs or trees, designed to emphasise the expansive sky above. After only a few moments there, I felt calm again.

Beside the garden stretched a wide lawn used as a bowling green. Although neither I in my cloth of silver gown nor my women in their fine summer livery were dressed for sports, I called for the wooden balls and cones. A game would provide a welcome distraction from my thoughts.

When the cones had been placed at the opposite ends of the green, I divided the women into two teams, and we began to play. But luck wasn't with me, and I played poorly, unable to throw the ball anywhere near the opposing cone. The women were quick to notice, and immediately started to throw in ways intended to mimic my poor performance, which only made me feel worse; I detested being so indulged.

When Anna, usually skilled and proficient at games, threw the ball so weakly it barely passed the halfway point on the green, I'd had enough. "You all treat me like a child!" I exploded. "Do you not think I notice how you are deliberately playing so badly?"

None of the women would look at my face, confirming my suspicions. "Do you think me such a fool as to not see what you do?"

Anna said, "Perhaps the restrictions of your dress are affecting you."

The remark only angered me further. "Oh!" I exclaimed, seizing the ball from the woman beside me and hurling it down the green. Everyone's eyes fixed on it as it sped along its course. It hit the cone forcefully and squarely in its centre, knocking it over. Instantly, there were delighted cries and applause from all the women. My mood improved, and I laughed.

Suddenly one of the women asked, "Who is that watching us from the garden?"

On the terrace was a stern-looking woman dressed in black, standing perfectly still and straight as a statue. So pronounced was the scowl of disapproval on her face, it was clearly visible from where we stood. Seeing us look at her, she stood her ground, staring back.

"It must be the Countess of Mar," I said, and started moving towards her, followed by the others. As I approached, I saw that her black gown, high-necked and severe beneath a white linen ruff, was of good silk and well fitted to her narrow form above the skirt. Her white hair was pulled back beneath a black cap, and she had deep-set wrinkles about her eyes, nose and mouth, and an unfriendly expression. It was as though a dead tree, bereft of leaves, had appeared in the vibrant garden, a jarring misfit that drew all attention.

When I reached her, she stood several feet above me on the terrace, and I had to look up. She made the feeblest attempt at a curtsey, half bowing her head. "Your Majesty," she said, in a strangely expressionless voice. "I am at your service."

"Welcome to court, Countess," I greeted her. "Your participation in the ceremony tomorrow will be most welcome."

She stared down at me, as though about to voice some withering criticism. I wished she had found me at some worthier activity than bowling. I felt like a child again, being scolded by my mother. "Thank you," she said finally, in a thin tone.

An awkward silence followed. Then I said, almost apologetically, "We were just enjoying ourselves. The reception of the English ambassador earlier was tedious and we needed something to improve the day."

She looked out beyond us to the bowling green, where the cones and balls still lay. Her expression softened as a distant look came to her eyes. "My son and the king used to play here," she said. Her words were heavy, conveying a lifetime of responsibilities and unhappiness.

I said, "Countess, you must be tired from your journey. Please, go and refresh yourself. Do whatever you need to make yourself comfortable."

She blinked. "Thank you," she replied plainly. She started to turn to leave, then remembered I was the queen, and stopped and began to walk backward.

"There's no need for that," I said quickly, smiling kindly at her. But the smile wasn't returned as she turned her back and left.

Behind me, one of the women giggled. Another said, "Countess of Mar? Doesn't 'mar' mean 'ruin'?" Beside me, Anna turned quickly, silencing them with a look.

The appearance of the countess had been like a grey cloud in the blue sky. But I was determined not to let it ruin the day. "Let us resume our game," I said, and led the way back to the green.

The countess didn't join us for dinner, sending a message shortly before noon asking to be excused, as she was indisposed after her trip. Dinner was being held in the large Outer Hall of James's apartments, since the Great Hall was being readied for the baptismal banquet the following day. The Great Hall was already legendary throughout Europe, due to its immense size and the golden render of the exterior walls. For the baptismal banquet, James was for once following in his grandfather's footsteps by embracing spectacle and display as statements of importance. He had planned an event that would be every bit as impressive as the building that held it, and workmen were still completing it. So, we were dining instead in his Outer Hall, a large and simply decorated room beneath a ceiling whose plain surface was mercifully devoid of carved wooden heads.

As soon as we were seated, I mentioned that I'd met the countess, but that she was presently resting from her trip. "I will look in on her later," I added, causing James to smile, reach over and place his hand on top of mine. I was glad we were back in accord again.

It was midafternoon by the time I made my way to the countess's room, in the older part of the castle where most of the guests who'd come for the baptism were staying. The rooms there were smaller and less grand than the newer palace, and not nearly as comfortable, but it was central enough for no one to feel marginalised or diminished by staying there.

I'd expected to find the countess in bed, but when her attendant showed me in, I found her fully dressed, seated upright at a table by an open window. She started to rise, but I stopped her. Clearly, she suffered from gout, and the day's travel had taken a toll on her bodily humours. I told the two women who'd accompanied me to wait in the hall, and went and sat down across from her. The view from the open window was breathtaking, as that part of the castle wall rose directly from the cliff beneath, and overlooked an extensive landscape that stretched for miles. It was almost impossible to avoid feeling power and authority, inspired by such a view.

A Bible she'd been reading lay open on the table. "The New Testament?" I asked.

"Matthew Five, Twenty," she said aridly. Then she quoted: "*For I tell you, unless your righteousness exceeds that of the Scribes and Pharisees, you will never enter the kingdom of heaven.*" She'd memorised it, and recited the text without looking down. Finishing, she stared at me with her small dark eyes, a self-satisfied look on her face.

I wasn't sure how to respond, or if I should even smile in agreement. I turned my face to the window, as though thoughtfully contemplating the verse. I wondered what had prompted her on this particular day, seated beside such an inspiring view, to linger over such bleak and stern words. The ugly thought that the answer was religious pomposity presented itself, but I pushed it away. The woman was to carry my child during the baptism tomorrow, and I wouldn't allow myself to think of her so.

I looked at her and said, "You must have many fond memories of being here at Stirling. Such a beautiful castle. The setting is awe-inspiring."

"I lived in the new part."

I couldn't tell if it was a rebuke for her not being housed there now, or just a comment, so I said apologetically, "We have so many guests now we couldn't fit everyone there."

"Those rooms are ostentatious." The wrinkles around her eyes deepened as she said the word 'ostentatious'. I had the distinct impression that she wondered if my English was sufficient to know what it meant. It was an attitude I sometimes still encountered, given my foreign birth, from those who didn't know I'd been taught English from early childhood, and had studied and practised it with a passion from the moment I arrived in Scotland. I suspected she had deliberately chosen to use a word I might not know, to establish a superiority over me.

"They certainly are elaborate," I answered. "Especially my own suite."

"I lived in them when I was one of Mary of Guise's women." She scowled distastefully. "They suited her."

"If you disliked her, why did you stay at her court?"

She stiffened, drawing herself back in the chair. Clearly, she wasn't used to being challenged, even on the simplest of matters. She waited a moment before replying. "Back then, my eyes hadn't been opened yet. It was some time before I grasped the truth of her nature; in fact, not until after she was dead. At the time, I thought she was very grand and generous, and I admired her — just as I admired her daughter when she first returned here."

Despite the woman's unfriendliness, I was still intrigued by her knowledge of the past. I'd encountered almost no one who had been close to either queen, and I wanted to know more. "You attended Mary Stuart also?"

"I was one of her closest companions. She liked me." She lifted her head as she said it, a look of pride on her face. It vanished as quickly as it had appeared, but no matter what she now said, it was clear she had thoroughly enjoyed those days as a companion to two queens of Scotland.

"Times of useless frivolity," she said sternly, adding darkly, "and worse."

Delicately, I said, "All the world knows that Mary Stuart couldn't clear herself of accusations of having conspired to murder Lord Darnley. But Mary of Guise I have never heard ill of. She struggled as regent to hold the Scottish throne for her daughter after she was sent to France."

"The House of Guise would stop at nothing to achieve their ambition," she said in a voice thick with dislike. "Even murder."

Shocked, I didn't want to hear any more. I changed the subject. "The king mentioned that his parents had fallen in love here at Stirling. I was surprised to hear him speak of them so, considering the conflict that developed between them. Can you tell me, is it true? Did they truly love each other, at first?"

The countess tilted her head slightly before replying. It had likely been years since she'd felt so important, and she was making the most of the opportunity. Then she sighed heavily, and said, "It appeared so, although with those two, who knew how deep it really ran? The truth was probably closer to them both feeling they could make use of the other. But Lord Darnley was as handsome as Mary was beautiful. He was polished and mannered and socially adept in ways that no one else around her in Scotland was. And for once, there was a man who stood as tall as she did." Her eyes narrowed shrewdly. "For her, it was also that she was older than him. I didn't think so at the time, but I saw it afterward. She thought she could control him, just as his mother had. She'd been older than her first husband, the French king, so she was used to it. When Darnley fell ill here at Stirling, she nursed him back to health, and it was then that they fell in love. Supposedly." She suddenly leaned in towards me, her eyes widening. "I can tell you that's how it goes! The love in the beginning turns into hate at the end." She said it as though imparting some great secret, and there was no question that she intended to suggest it would apply to my own marriage as well.

Slowly, and as gracefully as possible, I stood up, resisting the urge to run from the room. "Thank you for talking with me, Countess," I said with studied serenity. "But how rude I am, taking up so much of your time when you must be exhausted."

She started to rise also, but again, I stopped her. "I'll leave you in the best of company," I said, indicating the Bible.

"We must all strive to enter the kingdom of heaven," she called after me as I left. "It is good for you to know the past. Mr. Buchannan, the king's tutor when he was a child, would admonish his transgressions by reminding him of the nest of vipers from which he sprang."

The countess was a horrible woman, and not to be tolerated. In the hall, I told the women we were going at once to find the king, and started off at such a rapid pace they had trouble keeping up with me.

But by the time we reached the new palace, I'd thought better of confronting James over the countess. She'd only be present for the ceremony, and then would fade from my life as quickly as she'd appeared in it. James could not very well now retreat from having invited her participation, even if I did manage to convince him of how disturbing a person she had aged into. And I wouldn't have Henry's baptism, which promised to be a wonderful event, spoiled by quarrelling with James on the eve of it. No, it would be better for me to ignore the woman, and then let her just disappear.

That night James came to me as usual. "Anne," he breathed passionately as soon as the curtains had been drawn around us and he took me in his arms. I responded enthusiastically, running my fingers through his thick hair as he held me and kissed me. He must have been as affected by the baptism excitement as I was, feeling it a celebration of his virility as much as my fertility, and we coupled quickly and intensely.

Afterward, we both drank deeply from the jug of wine we were given at night, and he fell asleep not long after, one arm thrown over me. But I stayed awake longer, thinking of Mary of Guise, who had occupied the same room and grand state bed. The ambitions of the Guise had been well known throughout Europe. How many nights had that queen lain in this very bed, plotting and struggling to hold the Scottish throne for her child, and to bring her the English one? James was her grandson, and as he lay sleeping beside me, I wondered if the birth of his son might provoke the same ruthlessness in him. Although politically savvy and shrewd, I had never seen him ruthless.

He was already gone when I awoke in the morning, at the first signs of dawn. "An important day," said Anna, as she pulled back the bed curtains. "First light holds promise of it being fair."

I slid out of bed and we began the ritual of my dressing, simply, for prayers: the grand dress of white satin, brocaded with gold thread, and floral designs in thread of red and green, that I would wear for the ceremony and banquet that would come later. As Anna attended to me, I listened to the nurse's report of how Henry had passed his night, and fed, and his general temperament. So much of my life now revolved around him; he was in my thoughts from the first moments of my day.

The ceremony began later in the morning in my Inner Hall. I sat in my canopied chair of state, wearing my splendid dress, with a white silk cap far back on my head, a priceless pearl arrangement centred in my hair before it, touching my forehead. A large pearl dangled from each of my ears, with a pearl necklace, perfectly matched, about my neck. Everyone crowded into the room was also in rich and colourful finery, so that for once the immense unicorn tapestries hung high on the walls nearly faded into insignificance. The din of voices in my Outer Hall told me it too was packed to overflowing. Not since James's birth had Scotland celebrated the baptism of a prince, and the excitement pulsed throughout the very air of the palace.

The crowd hushed as the Countess of Mar, in black silk again, appeared from my bedroom, carrying Henry. She was followed by my women, all in crimson livery. The countess held Henry tightly in her arms and despite her age, I saw her grip was firm. Her face looked noble, much less unhappy than on the previous day. As she deftly placed Henry in the cradle beside me, bending with ease, I looked at her face, determined to smile if I caught her eye. But she never once looked towards me, and in the next moment she had stepped back with the other women, her part in the ceremony over. It had been but a moment, barely long enough for anyone to notice her, with all eyes on the prince, yet I was relieved it was done.

James's cousin, the Duke of Lennox, stepped forward beside the cradle and called out, "God save Prince Henry!" The cry was repeated throughout the hall, and echoed in the outer one, and somewhere further off trumpets sounded. Four Scottish lords came forward and stood in close attention as the duke lifted Henry from the cradle, and presented him to the young English earl. A canopy was unfolded and raised above the earl and Henry, and the procession began with the lords leading the way, the first carrying the ducal coronet of Rothsay, ahead of the earl, who held Henry sitting upright in the crook of his arm. I rose, my ladies falling in behind me, and we took our places. As we made our way out through the rooms of the palace to the chapel, everyone bowed and curtsied as we passed.

James, regal in a cloth of gold puffed and slashed doublet, matching slashed breeches, gold velvet cloak and wide-brimmed high hat, with feathers and a centrepiece of diamonds rivalling any crown, met us at the door to the chapel. He engaged in a ritual formal exchange with the English earl, with as much solemn deference as though his cousin Queen Elizabeth herself was present. Henry was then given back to the Duke of Lennox, who entered the chapel with James, walking down to where the Bishop of Aberdeen stood ready to perform the ritual. The rest of us filed in behind them, and found our places in the stalls. All were of bare wood, except that of James, which had been lined with golden velvet.

It has happened, I thought ecstatically as I watched the baptism unfold. *I have a son! I have a son, who will one day reign as king of Scotland and England.* I felt important in a way I never had. What a great thing it was to be a mother, to have produced a king from my own body! Pride and triumphant accomplishment coursed through me once more.

After the service we returned to my apartments, and Henry was placed in his cradle. I sat in the chair of state to receive the homage of ambassadors of various countries, and their gifts for Henry. The day felt as much a celebration of me as my son. Many precious jewels were pressed into my hands, more than I'd seen in my life, and other gifts of great value: a full set of plate; several enormous cups of gold from his godmother, Queen Elizabeth, which were so heavy they could barely be lifted; and a document granting Henry a yearly pension of five thousand florins, from the Dutch.

But the wonder I felt at the gifts was surpassed by that of the guests during the following feast in the Great Hall, which

James had laboured over for months. The first courses were rolled in on chariots by six women costumed in silver satin and tinsel as Ceres, Fecundity, Faith, Prosperity, Concord and Perseverance, and presented to the servers. Exclamations of delight rang through the hall at their appearance, but when the later courses were accompanied by the appearance of Neptune on a great moving ship, with a tall mast and lively waves on its side, the cries were of outright awe. Beside me on the dais, James sat in silence, quietly revelling in the success of what he had imagined and created. For the rest of the banquet the congratulations he received were as much for the success of the spectacular display as for the birth of Henry.

3

After the baptism we lingered at Stirling throughout the autumn and into the start of winter, differing from our customary change of residences. Councillors and government officials, and sometimes foreign visitors, arrived regularly, so much so that we did not feel remote at all from the capital. But in January, James told me he was needed in Edinburgh on important state business. "There will be receptions at which your presence is required," he told me. "We leave at the start of next week. Since I do not want Henry exposed to the winter weather, he is to remain here."

He said it smoothly, his blue eyes fixed on me. One of the few changes over the past months was his new moustache and small beard below his mouth. Both were neatly trimmed, and slightly fairer in colour than his hair, so there was no impression of gruffness. But they did make him look older, and the difference from the smoothness of his face when he kissed me had taken some time to adjust to.

As he looked at me, I caught a remote look in his eyes, but it passed, and his smile was serene yet engaging. I'd known the day would eventually come when I'd be separated from Henry for brief periods of time, due to situations such as the present one. Although I had increasingly dreaded the arrival of that day, I knew the time had come for me to adjust to it. Besides, Henry was flourishing. His wet nurse was no longer needed and had been dismissed a month ago, and right before Christmas he had delighted everyone by taking his first steps.

The winter had been cold and snowy, and there was no question Henry would be better off avoiding its harshness.

"Very well," I replied. "Anna can stay here in charge of Henry when we go. Surely no harm can come to him during the few weeks we will be gone."

His smile remained even. "Never forget he is a prince of Scotland, Anne," he said softly. "He must become used to all kinds of changes to ready him to take his place in the world."

Holyrood Palace was very different from Stirling Castle, and felt even more so for our having spent nearly a full year at Stirling. Low and spreading, it was less formidable, much less of a fortress, having evolved from an ancient monastery still adjacent to it. The monastery had been the most important religious site in Scotland prior to the Calvinists, and still cast a mystique about the palace. James's great-grandfather and grandfather had liked it and used it as their central seat, expanding the palace with a range of rooms around a central quadrangle, making it modern and comfortable, a place from which the business of a country could easily be attended to. The thriving commerce of the great city of Edinburgh at its front gates flowed into it, and, even with its pervasive air of religious connection, the palace felt very rich and luxurious in a way that Stirling Castle, for all its grandeur, did not.

I had lived at Holyrood Palace less than any of our residences, and when we arrived, I was shown to a suite of apartments I hadn't used before, on the upper floor of the northwest tower. In the oak ceiling were carved the initials of Mary of Guise, showing that they'd been used by her when she'd been queen. James's rooms were directly below, connected by a small circular stairway. The rooms were well appointed and charming, and after arriving my mood finally improved. It had plummeted following my separation from Henry; I had wept quietly for nearly the entire trip, barely able to hold back the tears even before the cheering crowds as we rode through the streets of Edinburgh. Only the thought of him with my faithful Anna — from whom I had extracted a thousand unnecessary promises to safeguard him — had made it bearable.

The first night at Holyrood, I supped alone with James in one of the small rooms of my suite used for dining. It was comfortable and cosy with its fire and candles holding back the cold and dark of the winter night. The food was excellently prepared, the several roast meats tender and seasoned. Life in the capital city held promise of all manner of interesting things, and I started to think of excursions with my women to the many shops of Edinburgh, and visits from the merchants. Despite the dour Calvinist influence, the city still offered as many sophisticated luxuries as the Copenhagen I'd known as a child, and there were artists and musicians. Henry, too, would need to encounter those things as I had, and I began to think it might be worthwhile to have him spend as much time as possible in the city as he grew.

As we ate, James and I talked of trivial things, him about recent competition among his gentlemen during a hunt, and me of some nonsense among my women practising a new dance. But over mulled wine and gingerbread, his talk became more serious, of the tensions between the Calvinist clergy and the remaining Catholic earls.

"The Earl of Huntley still refuses to renounce Catholicism," he said. "He ignored the suggestion that he leave the kingdom if he would not. The clergy are now insisting he be banished."

James sat across from me, his hands clasped together just below his bearded chin, his fingers interlocked. His fingertips rubbed continuously against the knuckles of his other hand, but in the flickering light of the candelabras his face looked unperturbed.

It was rare he spoke of politics to me, and I couldn't understand why he now would. Yet I knew him well enough to know he never said anything without intent; his childhood had taught him it could be dangerous. For some reason, he wanted to engage me on the matter, or at least let me know his opinion.

"It's because he was found conspiring with the Spanish, is it not?" I asked. "Not just because he clings to the old religion?"

James waved a hand dismissively. "The Spanish conspiracy was nonsense. It's been this way for years now with the lords who are Catholic, or suspected of it. Charges of treason, excommunications, attainders. The truth is that the clergy want all the lords to convert. They wish to completely stamp out Romanism in this kingdom. It has been like this since John Knox brought back the ways of Calvin from Switzerland when my grandmother was regent. When my mother returned from France, she stepped into the worst of the struggle."

The story was one of turmoil, disastrous decisions, and ruin. But the way James spoke of it was oddly devoid of that heaviness, and his posture and demeanour showed no shift towards the exhaustion that might have been expected from a lifetime of such a burden. Instead, he looked perfectly composed and confident. He said, "She failed to understand such forces can keep each other in check, and prevent them from turning their combined strength on a ruler. I am not averse to balancing differing factions in my kingdom, religious-based or otherwise. The lords respect me and my abilities. I am in concord with the clergy on religious doctrine. We have reached a balance."

He leaned back in his chair, stretching his hands out in front of him, palms outward, fingers still interlocked. "But you must be ever vigilant; you must never let your guard down, or the balance will be lost. You must understand this, Anne. You must be ever aware of the shifting nature of power, and that there are those who will try to take what is yours from you, in whatever way they can." He paused, then repeated, "You must understand this, Anne."

The firelight on the tapestries lining the walls of the little room seemed to cast a pall of danger over the bucolic scenes depicted. "I do," I answered quickly. "You forget, I was raised at the court of the Danish king."

"Denmark," he said softly, "has never been as factious as Scotland." He dropped his hands to the arms of the chair, grasping them. "But you are astute. You have seen the religious struggle here."

"What becomes of the Earl of Huntley?"

"I understand he is readying to leave the kingdom. If so, there will be no need for me to banish him. But it remains to be seen what course the other Catholic lords will take."

His view of the religious struggle as a conflict to be managed and not overcome was troubling. In the past, he had spoken of his ambitions to bring religious and political peace not only to Scotland and England, but to all of Europe as well. Something had shifted in him.

James abruptly changed the subject. "These were the rooms that my mother occupied here. My father's were directly below." A tiny fear touched me, very small and quick, like when a pin from a garment comes undone and causes a scratch. I'd seen the initials of Mary of Guise in the ceiling in the bedroom, but I hadn't known that her daughter had used the suite also. For an instant, I could almost feel Mary Stuart's ghost in the room beside me. Long ago I had once been told that it was at Holyrood that her marriage to Lord Darnley had collapsed. But it was something I hadn't remembered until James had just now brought it up.

Looking around the room, he continued, "It was right here that David Rizzio was stabbed to death."

Part of me didn't want to hear what would follow. But James sat silently, his heavy-lidded eyes watching me, until I asked, "Who was this Mr Rizzio?"

"My mother's secretary. An Italian. A group of Calvinist lords felt he was influencing her against them. They also wanted to show who was truly in charge in Scotland."

I managed to take another sip of the mulled wine. But the cinnamon in it no longer tasted so sweet, and the cloves were bitter. "The poor man," I murmured. "Where was the queen that she couldn't protect him?"

"She was here," he said with strange mildness. "They were at supper. When the conspirators burst in, he tried to hide behind her while she argued, saying the Scottish Parliament would punish Rizzio if it found he had offended. But they dragged him out, pointing a wheellock pistol at her belly. At me, too; she was in her seventh month."

I gasped and nearly dropped my wine cup. He, with perfect composure, continued, "They murdered him in front of her, and dragged his body out and threw it down the stairs."

"What a horror!" I finally managed to say. "But where was your father, that he couldn't protect her?"

James reached forward and laid a finger on his own cup. From the shadows by the door a servant emerged and refilled it. "Wait outside with the others," James told him, his tone abrupt. The sound of the wooden door shutting behind the man sounded heavy and final.

James lifted his newly filled cup but didn't drink from it, holding it poised before him. In the same mild tone, he said,

"My father was present, with the conspirators. They'd promised to make him king, which my mother had refused to do. He threw in his lot with him even though they were Calvinists, and he and my mother Catholics. And I'm told he didn't just watch. He stabbed Rizzio also. It's said it was his dagger plunge that killed him."

Speechless, I sat staring at James as he lifted the cup to his lips and drank from it. Then he went on, "That was the beginning of the end of their marriage. Oh, my mother patched it up quickly enough — she was always shrewder than my father, and she dissembled to draw him back to her, until I was born. Seemingly, they were still reconciled when he was — " he hesitated — "murdered." James set the cup down on the table. "But my mother wasn't the type of woman to ever get over something like that. I'm sure she hated him."

The Countess of Mar had told me that when young, James had been taught that he sprang from a nest of vipers. Since childhood, I, along with everyone else in Europe, had heard the tale that Mary Stuart had likely had Lord Darnley murdered. But I'd never heard of the misfortunes leading up to it, which now gave credence to the theory. Overwhelming sympathy for James overcame my horror at the thought of his having had a loaded pistol pointed at him shortly before his birth, while only a few feet away his father had helped stab to death one of his mother's companions. Even a viper's nest would not have been so ugly. "A terrible tale," I finally managed to say.

"Yes. It is." He stood up. Fear clawed at me; there was more.

He flicked his sleeve as though to shake crumbs off it, and said, "So you see, Anne, Scotland can be a very dangerous place, especially troubled as it is with religious discord. There are always those who will try to manipulate it and take our power away. We must stand together, and not allow anyone to take advantage of any seeming discord between us."

"Certainly," I agreed. "Haven't we always?"

"We must now protect our son."

"What else can we do?"

Without the slightest hesitation, he answered, "He is to have his own household at Stirling Castle, separate from ours. It is the most secure of our castles, and easily defended. It was why I was kept there as a child." His gaze had remained fixed on me as he'd said it, his expression blank. But now he half-smiled. "Very successfully, you see, as I sit here before you, sound of body."

It took an instant for the implication of what he was saying to impress itself upon me. As it did, my back grew rigid. "You mean you wish Henry to be separated from us?" I asked with incredulity.

"Yes. It is the surest way of safeguarding him."

"That's impossible, James! He needs to be with his mother!"

"Anne, you must be thoughtful. Our son must be in an environment devoted exclusively to his well-being. You and I have too many other distractions involved in the carrying out of our responsibilities as sovereigns. There are too many comings and goings at court, too many people we can't oversee. We must do what is best for him, and that is for him to live and be raised apart from us, at Stirling."

I was so stunned by what James was proposing, it was almost impossible to think clearly. My entire body had begun to tremble from a combined fear and anger as I refrained from shouting a fierce and bitter refusal. *Time*, I thought. *Gain time to prevent it and find a way to stop it permanently*. My wine cup was still in my hand, and any moment my trembling would be apparent.

With enormous effort I held it steadily as I set it down on the table.

"Perhaps when he is a little older," I said.

Smoothly, he replied, "It is already arranged. Henry will remain at Stirling. His household has already been formed. They arrive this week."

My child, suddenly surrounded by strangers, was impossible to accept. Out of my outrage, one clear thought sprang, which I voiced: "Thank God Anna is still there with him."

"She is right now on her way to rejoin you here. Henry must have those attending him who are experienced enough to do so."

"And who might that be?" I demanded.

"The Earl of Mar has been appointed governor. His mother is governess."

For a moment I wasn't sure I'd heard correctly. Appalled, I could barely whisper, "The Countess of Mar?"

"Yes. The Countess of Mar is to have charge of him."

My fingers clenched into a fist and I smashed it down on the table. "No!" I shouted.

James flinched — he'd never seen me so before — and his eyes widened. He said, "You must be thoughtful —"

I interrupted him by standing up. Then I laughed, harshly and ruefully. "Thoughtful?" I asked. "It is I who am being sufficiently thoughtful, not you. Have your thoughts become deranged, James? To even suggest that I would consider giving over the care of my son to that horrid old creature is an abomination!"

"She is an upright and honest woman," he replied, for the first time with tension in his voice. "She and her son are two of the only people in this entire kingdom I have full trust in. You must not speak of so valuable a subject in that way."

"She is a bitter and angry woman, ugly of heart and nature! I question how her son could be much different, having been so long in her company!"

Coldly, he said, "Madam, you are speaking of one of my oldest and closest friends."

"One who has obviously influenced you in the most negative of ways, sir."

One of his hands sprang up, and he pointed to me. "Sit down. Your stance is not only unseemly, but foolish."

"Better than your attitude regarding the well-being of your child, which is the same."

His anger got the better of him; it was his turn to stand. "Let me remind you, Your Majesty, that you are the queen!"

"And let me remind *you* that you are the king!" Never had I spoken to him so, or anyone, in many years, for never since childhood had my anger reached such expression. I'd been taught that a princess never indulged in such unbecoming displays. Anger, when I'd felt it, had been shown in measured, careful responses. But I was now past the point of caring. Hand in hand with my outrage over his proposed separation from my child, and the placing of him in the care of a woman I despised, was an appalling feeling of betrayal. James had known I would not agree to such a change and had proceeded with it anyway. My feelings and desires had been placed second for him, which he had never done before during our marriage. Something had drastically changed between us, or was hovering on the verge of doing so, and unless I could prevent it, I feared our marriage would never be the same. It was urgent that I made him see the extent of my disturbance.

He stood across the table from me, his breathing strong with agitation, his expression angry in a way I'd never seen before. It also held a look of extreme surprise, telling me he hadn't expected opposition to this extent. It gave me an advantage, and I took it. "It baffles me completely that you could even imagine I would consent to such an arrangement," I said strongly. "You say we must do what is best for the prince, and certainly that would be for him to remain in proximity to the love of his parents. At least, until he is older." Even in my anger I saw it had been a mistake to attack the Countess of Mar. "I am sure your friends have qualities to recommend them, but no matter how fine, nothing can compare with a mother's love."

It was his turn to laugh, but instead of harsh and loud, it was low and drawn out. Then he said vehemently, "Speak not to me, madam, of a mother's love!"

I started to speak, but James stopped me by raising both of his hands. "Enough!" he exclaimed. He drew a deep breath and appeared to collect himself. Then, with a frosty calmness, he said, "The prince needs to be in the care of those not guided by their feelings. Your outburst here today, and your continuing refusal to view the matter with careful deliberation, supports this decision. Henry needs to be with those who can evaluate all matters pertaining to his care without being coloured by personal attachment." His tone changed, becoming softer. "I am sorry, Anne, that this is such a great shock to you. But I am sure you will shortly come to see the wisdom of it."

"Never!" I exploded. I seized my silver wine cup and hurled it away, the contents spilling out before it hit the floor with a metallic thud. "Tomorrow I am going to ride back to Stirling and take charge of the prince myself!"

"No," he said sternly.

"Yes! And perhaps, James, I should then take the prince across the sea to Denmark, where my brother is able to protect him from so strange a parent! And me from so unappreciative a husband."

Too late, I knew I'd gone too far. I'd threatened him politically, with implications for the kingdom, something I had never done before. I had inadvertently moved the entire argument to a different, more dangerous, arena.

James's expression became unreadable, like a book being closed. Without another word he turned to leave. I knew I should call after him, to make some effort to repair the rift between us, but my own anger would not let me. I was the queen, his equal, and he had treated me as though I were not.

The door opened as he neared it; the attendants on the other side must have been listening for his footsteps. If so, they would have heard the entire exchange between us as well. Tomorrow, all the court would know of it. With a sinking sensation, I realised the extent to which it had been a mistake to so overtly argue with him.

The door closed behind him, and I was left alone, staring at the cup on the floor and the spilled wine beside it. If James's intent had been to deliberately destroy our marriage, there was no more suitable place in all of Scotland for him to have chosen than the room where his parents' marriage had so bloodily unravelled.

I had a sleepless night, alternately crying into my pillow in despair and angrily assembling plans, all of which seemed full of grand potential at first but within minutes collapsed into futility.

The knowledge that Mary Stuart had likely spent as wretched a night in that same bed after seeing her husband participate in the death of her secretary seemed at the same time both repellent and fitting.

In the morning, I refused to rise from the bed. "I am not well," I told the women. "Send a message to the king telling him so."

A message came back saying he was sorry to hear so, but trusted in my speedy recovery. He would alert the court physicians I would be calling for them.

The women asked if they should send for the physicians. "You should not!" I nearly shrieked at them. "I will lie here until I die!" And I yanked the bed curtains closed around me, and wept copiously again. Finally, exhausted, I slept.

When I awoke, I lay in bed silently, wondering what the hour was. Utter silence prevailed in the room beyond the bedcurtains, an emptiness matching the void I felt within me every time I thought of Henry. It felt impossible that the present situation could be true. I berated myself for not having seen the signs of it sooner, which surely must have been there. If I'd known of the plans before leaving Stirling, I simply would have refused to depart. But I now saw that James must have anticipated that I would have responded so, and thus had shrewdly decided to remove me before letting me know.

Beyond the curtains, I heard a door open, and then voices in the bedroom. Then, suddenly, the curtains at the foot of the bed were pulled back, revealing Anna standing there, dressed in a fur cape and hood. Instantly, I burst into tears. Everything was true. My son was now alone at Stirling, in the care of the hideous Countess of Mar.

Anna came around to the side of the bed and pulled back the curtains. "It's time to get up now, Your Grace," she said plainly.

She stood so close to the side of the bed I could feel the coldness of her cape, and see the traces of snow on the fur. She must have ridden hard to get here, thinking she'd be the one to give me the unfortunate news. But upon arriving at the palace she must have learned that I already knew.

"How is my son?" I asked, sitting up.

"Thriving."

"I can't stand to think of him in the care of that dreadful woman! I didn't want to leave him even in your care!"

Anna pushed off her hood and undid her cloak, tossing it on the foot of the bed. Then she sat down beside me and took my hands in hers. Hers were cold, distracting me from my own woes. "You're freezing!"

"It is snowing. We had trouble making our way through it, or I would have been here sooner. I knew the news would be devastating for you. But, madam, you must control yourself. The change is unfortunate, but not disastrous. The child continues in good health. And his care changes little. All of his attendants remain the same, except for your presence, and that of your women. He will barely be aware of the Countess of Mar. Some days it is likely he will not see her at all."

"Even that is too much!" I buried my face in my hands. "It is an outrage, Anna!" I grasped the edge of a blanket in my fists.

She didn't reply, knowing it would be dangerous for her to voice criticism of the king or his policies. But her face, I saw as I dropped my hands, showed she was in agreement with me. Quietly, she said, "I have prayed the entire way here, for guidance. Prayed to Mary, the holy mother of Jesus. You must think of the great fortitude she showed when she was parted from her son."

I leaned back and tried to offer a prayer, but it did no good. I remained angry, and felt no clearer about what to do. The only thought that came was of the religious sternness of the Countess of Mar, and that Henry would grow up under such supervision.

"James's childhood was unhappy in the care of that woman," I said. "Her harshness and what he was taught took a toll on him that still lingers today. I do not want my son raised so. Neither should James. It baffles me that he has chosen to remove the child from my care. I don't understand why he would treat him so. And even less, why he would do something so cruel and degrading to me. It's a statement for all the world that he does not feel me competent to have the care of my own child. I tell you, it's an insult not to be stood!"

"No insult was intended to you. The custom is different here in Scotland than it is in Denmark. There, the royal children are raised in the household of the king and queen. But here, each royal child has his own."

"You mean that each child I give birth to will be taken from me? That I shall not be allowed to raise any of them?"

"It is the tradition here, of many years' standing."

"How do you know this?" I demanded, not wanting to believe it, but knowing that of all people, I could trust her the most.

"The Earl of Mar explained it to me. When they arrived at Stirling, he and his mother at once called me to them and broke the news of the changes. I must tell you, madam, they were very civil, and he was even kind. His way is gentler, more personable, than that of his mother. He told me that such has been Scottish tradition for centuries, and that the king could not break with it without trouble, even were he inclined to. He also recognised it would be difficult for you when you learned of it, and he urged me to do what I could to ease your adjustment."

"Which you are now doing," I said pointedly, and with bitterness. Her face changed; I had wounded her. Guilt clawed at me, and I reached out and grasped her hands. "Don't abandon me, Anna! I couldn't abide another loss."

"Never," she said resolutely.

For the first time I noticed how tired she looked. I pushed past her and got out of bed, calling for the women. "What time is it?" I asked Anna, and she answered it was past midday.

The women entered, one of them carrying a heavy robe which she threw over my shoulders, another with a pair of fur-lined slippers for my feet. I told them to bring food for Anna and me to dine. Several of them hurried out to get it. One of the remaining women timidly stepped forward and said the king had just sent an attendant to enquire after my health. I replied, "Tell him the queen says her heart has been broken."

The woman remained in place as though rooted to the floor, her eyes wide, the colour draining from her face. "Go," I said. "Take him the message yourself!" She turned and ran from the room, while the others stood in place, eyes averted, hands clasped before them.

To them, I said, "What use is pretence? All of you must know by now that the king has separated me from the prince. Soon, all of Europe will know, too. So, you are all to see what follows when I am treated wrongly. And Europe, as well!"

Some of the women started sobbing. Two of the younger ones came forward and fell on their knees before me, hugging my legs. Anna whispered, "More composure at this time."

The women were frightened, never having seen me so, or any sign of trouble between me and the king. It wasn't right for me to behave so. I helped the ones at my feet stand up, and then shooed them all away to the outer receiving room. Then I took Anna by the arm and led her to the table by the window. The shutters and curtains were opened, but there was no sunlight, and outside only shifting curtains of snow. I said, "It looks as though the very heavens have collapsed and are falling down around us."

Later, after we'd dined, I felt stronger, better able to contend with the appalling predicament. Anna's news of the mild disposition of the Earl of Mar, and that Henry's attendants were largely unchanged, had helped quiet my fears for his comfort and safety, and the information that the arrangement was traditional in Scotland also made my position feel less demeaning. But I still could not accept it. I felt as though a piece of my soul was being wrenched away, and if I did not get it back, I would be forever diminished. The experience of having given birth to my son had changed me permanently, and there could be no going back to how I had been before.

James's betrayal was shocking, and all the more because I had always been sure of his love for me. The anger I felt was surpassed by my confusion. Something had happened that I didn't understand, but had dealt me a double blow of the loss of both husband and son. The two losses were linked, and it was imperative for me to recover both. But I had no idea how to do it.

"I'm going to remain secluded for a while," I said to Anna. "I can't be around the king until I am absolutely certain of what course I should steer. But one thing I know is it will accomplish nothing for me to angrily confront him." I remembered how I'd threatened to take Henry to Denmark. "I have said too much already. My silence, and withdrawal, should make him understand the extent of my feelings. And it may impress on him how it feels to be isolated and alone. But I tell you this: I am going to have my son back."

I looked out the window; the falling snow had continued unabated. "Do you know, Anna, that these were the rooms where James's mother lived? And his father occupied those below, where he is now. I don't like it. It feels a bad sign that this is where this breech between us occurred."

"Ignore it," she said, dismissively. "That is meaningless for you."

"His parents' marriage never recovered from what happened here. Even the birth of a boy wasn't enough for them to overcome it."

"Mary Queen of Scots," Anna said plainly, "had hate in her. It is said she grew to hate Lord Darnley, and he her. But you, madam, are not such a creature as to make a way of hate. And neither is the king."

After a moment, I said, "I don't think I could ever hate James. But I hate what he did in taking my child from me. Hopefully things will change before love turns to hate."

As I stared out the window at the snow, the knowledge that I might come to hate the man I still loved was terrifying, and nearly impossible to accept. But the loss of my son was unbearable.

I remained in my rooms, nursing my grievances and biding my time. I wondered how James was feeling, if he felt as wretchedly lonely in his rooms directly below as I did in mine. Every night, when the curtains were drawn around me, I would be overcome with a feeling of emptiness that even anger could not successfully distract me from. And then, in the morning, when the curtains were drawn back and I emerged from the bed, came the times when I missed Henry the most. Surely, he knew I was no longer there. My presence in his daily routine hadn't been constant, but he must have recognised the importance of my appearances, and the significance of who I was to him. It was with distaste that I thought those feelings had now been shifted to the stern and dour Countess of Mar. To 'mar', someone had said, meant to 'ruin', and the countess's appearance in my life had certainly lived up to her title.

4

Two weeks of seclusion later, in the morning when the women drew back the bed curtains, I told them I would join the king at prayers. I had formulated my plan; now the day had come for me to put it into action. "Bring me my new soft blue damask gown," I told the women. "The new one with the light pink embroidery, that the king hasn't seen me in yet. And find one of the lighter coloured cloaks to go with it, one of the lined wool ones, so I don't freeze in that old church. But I'm not wearing furs today. The king hasn't laid eyes on me for two weeks, and I want to look like a breath of spring on this cold winter day." I ran a hand through my thick hair. "We need to spend much time on my hair, too. I want it to look as fair and shining as possible, so bring all the hairbrushes. I must look the way the sky does after a long day of rain clouds has cleared."

As they hurried away to gather everything, Anna remained, looking at me intently, her blue eyes focused and questioning. I said confidently, "My husband is going to do as I want. I merely need to remind him that he loves me. He may have lost his way — briefly. I will help him find it again."

I felt differently towards James, still angry and betrayed. The absence of Henry had left a void in the centre of my life, not searing as the anger had at first been, but more frightening in its dull emptiness. Some central part of me that had been so vibrantly awakened by his birth had been erased. For all that I was a queen, fawned over and made much of, I felt diminished, unimportant. My self-imposed isolation had increased my feeling of irrelevance, widening the void of Henry's absence, and I worried that I would be driven mad. I had therefore decided to emerge from seclusion, which I had intended to maintain for at least a month. It was time to embark on a new course of action. There was no reason why I couldn't recover what had been lost. If James and I regained our footing, in time the lingering ugly feelings would surely vanish, and we could move forward on the same path we'd been on, side by side, our son with us.

The abbey church at Holyrood had years earlier been altered to suit the Calvinist ways, and in addition to the pulpit replacing the altar, many of the wonderful old stained-glass windows had been sealed over. But the updates hadn't succeeded in completely eliminating the underlying glory and beauty of the old Catholic religious style. The church was connected to the rear of the palace, and despite its modern austerity, it still felt very ancient and old, and linked to the very heart of the royal family, justifying its power through the approval of God.

James and his attendants were already seated when I entered, followed by my women. They'd been alerted we were coming; it had been a long walk from my rooms on the other side of the palace, and fleet-footed servants had done their job well in getting the news to James that I had emerged from my rooms. A loud whisper arose as those in the pews looked back at us as we made our way down to my place in the front, across from James. He didn't look back, but as I reached the front, he turned to me and stood. Mixed feelings of sadness and resentment over what had occurred, and happiness at seeing him again, tore at me, but I kept my composure. His expression was perfectly controlled, giving no clue as to his response to my appearance. Facing each other, we both bowed slightly in acknowledgement. Then we both took our seats.

Very lightly, I breathed a sigh of relief at having accomplished the first step. Part of me had still been unsure as to whether or not my emotions would get the better of me upon seeing him, provoking some unexpected response from me. But the formality and dignity of the abbey church had lent themselves to restraint.

Afterward, upon leaving, James and I repeated our same dignified acknowledgements of each other, and left with our separate attendants to breakfast in our individual apartments. We were there for no more than a few minutes when a message came from him, stating how pleased he was with my recovery. At mid-morning he was to receive the Dutch ambassadors in the throne room, and would be further pleased for me to join him there. I sent back a message that I would; the first part of my plan was succeeding.

When I appeared, the room was packed with courtiers, news having spread through the palace that I had reappeared. All of them, I well understood, knew of the estrangement between James and myself, and its cause, and were eager to see what form our reconciliation would take, or if indeed there would be none. The court always observed us closely, gossiping and speculating. It was the way of it for a royal family, to be the focus of such attention, and I was as used to it as James was. But for the first time I found it intrusive and annoying. Never had so much been at stake for me, and to have to initiate a plan requiring extreme subtlety and delicacy under such minute court observation made me resentful as well as anxious.

All faces turned to me as I entered at the rear of the room, and began my way down the aisle towards the thrones where James was already seated. But unlike in the church earlier, everyone bowed or curtsied, a rippling wave of faces and heads dipping and rising on either side of me as I passed. James stood as I reached him, and came forward and took my hand to lead me to my throne. As soon as I was seated, the entire room burst into applause. I was taken by surprise, not by the applause, which I'd heard many times before, but by finding that I relished it as much as I did. The walk down the aisle had also given me a new and unfamiliar satisfaction. Suddenly the scrutiny of the staring faces no longer felt unpleasant and unwanted, but instead, something to be valued. The frightening emptiness within me felt a little smaller. Nothing could make up for the loss of my son, but somehow being the admired centre of attention helped to make it just a little more bearable.

James sat down again, with a heaviness I'd never noticed before during the countless times we'd taken our thrones in our several palaces. His expression as he'd led me to mine had been indecipherable, as I'd expected it would be. But he looked older; there were little frown lines in his forehead, and a slight heaviness about his cheekbones. *His youth is starting to leave him*, I thought. I wondered if the signs had always been there, or if they'd been brought about by the rift with me.

He hadn't smiled, or given any sign that my appearance was anything other than routine, and completely expected. He too had long ago mastered the art of showing the prying eyes of the courtiers as little as possible of what he truly felt. The flick of a finger, the wave of a hand, the slightest smile or frown would be seized on by them and interpreted — correctly or not — in an attempt to gain an advantage in finding favour with us.

James now gratified all of them by reaching over and placing his hand over mine, which was resting on the arm of the throne closest to him. It was an outright statement of unity and affection between us. I could count on the fingers of one hand how many times he had ever done so in such a formal, public setting. For an instant, I thought of Henry, far away at Stirling Castle, the stern Countess of Mar in her black dress leaning over him, and anger surged within me. I fought back the temptation to yank my hand away, for all the court to see. A display of anger would not get me what I wanted. I turned my face towards his; seeing it, he did the same. I smiled, forcing it at first, but as I caught a glimpse of his blue eyes beneath the heavy lids, the love I still felt for him made it genuine. For all that he had wounded me deeply and caused me unimaginable distress, I still loved him, and I was sure he still loved me. I would regain my son by getting him to understand the child should live surrounded by such love, and not sternness.

For the rest of the day I remained by his side, first through the audience with the Dutch ambassador, and then dinner. In the afternoon, wrapped in furs, we walked through the snow-covered gardens of Holyrood, dazzlingly white in the brilliant afternoon sunlight. Then we went back inside to resolve a quarrel brought to James by a group of contentious Edinburgh merchants. Supper followed, and then there was music from the best of the city's musicians, better than anything we had heard at Stirling.

Of course, James came to me that night. "Anne," he breathed as he took me in his arms, and his lovemaking was passionate and quick, and repeated during the night. I welcomed it, and felt more myself than I had for the past weeks. But something was different about it; it felt more serious and important, and not as spontaneous as in the past. His body felt heavier to me, and he seemed older, in the same way I had noticed in the throne room. I wondered if the changes had been occurring for some time, and were now only apparent because of his recent absence.

In the morning, Anna asked me if we'd spoken of the prince. "Not once," I replied. "We spoke of nothing of consequence all day, as if by agreement. It's too soon for me to talk to him about Henry. I have to be patient, and let our quarrel fade into the past. But I will have my child with me again!"

"I will pray not only to the mother of our Lord," she offered, "but to her mother, St Anne. Since we bear her name, she will surely hear me. And I'll pray to St Elizabeth, the mother of his cousin, the Baptist."

Anna's Catholic leanings were becoming more pronounced; she was now praying not only to Mary, but to saints. I was about to caution her against it, but stopped. There was more colour in the old religion, and her prayers brought her closer to it, allowing her to touch things absent in her own life.

"Anna, isn't it time we found a husband for you?"

She tensed, becoming entirely still. Her answer was plain and simple: "No."

"Have you no desire for a child of your own?"

"My place is here." She said it cheerfully, looking directly at me and smiling. But although her blue eyes were wide, there was a fixed look about them, and her smile was a bit too broad. She abruptly turned to the other women, called one by name, and hurried away to her, letting me know she wanted no further questions. Something about marriage frightened her and she had retreated from it, choosing to experience it from a distance through me. After the turmoil my husband had just subjected me to, I wasn't sure I should urge her towards a different path. If she found comfort and meaning in the Catholic ways, I would not deter her from them, so long as she continued to be cautious in their expression.

Later that morning, an Edinburgh goldsmith arrived with an array of jewellery for me to choose from as a gift from the king. I met him in the outer reception room, pleased at this additional sign of James's satisfaction over our reconciliation, but not particularly interested in the jewellery, which I'd never had more than a mild appreciation of.

The goldsmith was younger than I'd expected, in his early thirties, and tall and slender with fair hair, a long face and large, expressive brown eyes. His name, he said, was George Heriot; he stated that he was a burgess of the city, and a member of the Incorporation of Goldsmiths. His voice was pleasingly soft and mild. The hands with which he unwrapped and spread out a long piece of white silk on the table before me, were more those of an artist than an artisan, with long, well-shaped fingers.

With the precision of a musician playing an instrument, he arranged several jewels on the silk. All were intricate and dazzling, beautifully wrought, and an unfamiliar excitement stirred within me with each new one that appeared. There was a gold necklace set with repeating sequences of diamonds and rubies, and another of gold only, multiple delicate chains formed together, and another of perfectly matched pearls. There were gold-set diamond rings of various design, and bracelets, one jewel-covered, and another of two hands clasped together. Most interesting were the brooches, two of them, one gold and in the shape of a lion's head, the other a heart of rubies, surrounded by gold.

"Beautiful workmanship," I commented to Mr Heriot, who stood silently by my side as I examined them.

"I've been creating since childhood," he replied in his soft voice. "My father taught me. I take great satisfaction in shaping things both beautiful and of much value."

My admiration and appreciation of the display of jewels magnified, and I had a sudden urge to scoop them up and adorn myself with all of them. The feeling was new to me, and surprising. The knowledge that one of the pieces would be mine was gratifying in a way I'd never felt before.

"Never have I been so satisfied with jewellery to choose from, Mr Heriot," I said. "I find it almost impossible to make a choice." I turned sideways to look at him, and saw that he was smiling. *Perhaps he'll let me keep them all*, I was surprised to find myself thinking. Even were he to offer them, I couldn't accept the gift, either from the king or from him as an artisan seeking further patronage. It wasn't right for anyone to take advantage of those seeking their favour. Besides, I was wealthy enough to buy all of the jewels myself if I wanted to. I was likely the richest woman in Scotland, for in addition to what I'd received in Scottish residences and properties upon my marriage, I had inherited much from my father.

With a little wave of my hand I beckoned the women to come forward. Like a flock of geese they swooped over from the side of the room, where they'd barely been able to contain their excited curiosity, and clustered around the table, exclaiming in delight. Most of them favoured the necklace of the varied gems, and urged me to choose it. But I had already decided upon the heart-shaped brooch of gold and rubies. I had preferred the gold brooch in the shape of a lion's head, but given the circumstances of the gift, it would be better luck to choose the heart.

After a few minutes, I shooed the women away. "I like the heart," I told Mr Heriot.

"A wise choice, Your Grace," he said softly. "I am not surprised. I was told you favoured the colours red and white. I guessed you would choose either pearls or rubies." He began to gather up the other pieces.

"In truth, I like everything you have shown me — very much. Something about your craftsmanship appeals to me in ways others have not. I intend to patronise you further, when my purse allows it. But that purse isn't as large as one would expect a queen's to be. Scotland's resources are limited."

He took up the last piece, leaving only the ruby and gold brooch on the white silk. Although still beautiful, it looked lonely on the sea of white. I said, "But England is a country of vast and almost unlimited wealth." At once, I was shocked that I would utter aloud what had been a passing thought, especially to someone who was barely more than a stranger. It was something I never did; I was always extremely careful of what I said. And it was important to be even more so regarding anything about England, where we had such hopes for the future.

Mr Heriot finished collecting his jewellery, deftly sliding the remaining brooch off the silk and onto the table, where it looked even more vibrant against the dark wood. He appeared to have taken no notice of my remark, and looked intent on wrapping up the white silk. I decided to say nothing more; I couldn't think of a mitigating comment. Besides, I didn't know his political views, or whose patronage he enjoyed, or what religious beliefs he favoured. His working with luxury items would lend one to believe he favoured the old Catholic ways, but his clothing, although made of excellent wool and well-tailored, was a solid dark grey, and plain like a Calvinist's. Better for me to say nothing, neither advancing or retreating from what I'd said about England.

Finishing wrapping the silk, he looked at me and smiled. "Scotland isn't so rich," he said. "Especially not with ready money. I am aware, Your Majesty, that your own considerable wealth is largely in lands. My occupation gives me access to much money. I am at your service should you ever require a loan, or wish to convert some of your holdings into money."

I knew that goldsmiths worked this way at times. The man was honest, and hadn't tried to sell me further pieces. A month ago I wouldn't have paid any attention to his offer to help me find money should I need it, but now it felt valuable to know someone with such an ability. One needed power to work one's will, and power came from money, even more than hereditary social positions or titles. It also came from associates, from being surrounded by others who could combine their influence to achieve a desired result. Mr Heriot might be able to help me a great deal with my future plans, if needed. The problem with James had improved, and showed signs of continuing to do so. It was likely only a matter of weeks, or months at most, before Henry was back in my care again. But the past month had taught me not to be overly sure of what the future held; the separation from my child had been an abrupt and ugly surprise. Should things not go as I intended, or should there be further surprises, I might have to marshal my resources, and having access to a large amount of money could be important.

"Mr Heriot, your visit here today has been most satisfactory. I am surprised I haven't made your acquaintance sooner."

"You have not been much in Edinburgh, madam. And King James has never shown interest in the trinkets I have to offer."

"The king has no taste for fine things," I answered. "Partly this is by nature, and partly it is how he was taught. He values books and learning. And hunting, of course. One's husband influences one's choices in so many ways, even for a queen. I like hunting, but I've never been a scholar."

"You speak English like a native. And I'm told you write a perfect hand. Remarkable feats, and not accomplished by one without a powerful intellect." He said this quietly, without a trace of flattery. He had no need to flatter me, being secure in his own estimation as someone who excelled at what he did, with a certainty that he could rely on it to carry him through life. His brown eyes as he looked at me were frank, and without a taste for intrigue. He would be a valuable associate who wouldn't try to use me for his own advantage.

"Unlike the king," I said, "I find what you offer exceptional. They are far from trinkets, much more works of art. Now that I have seen them, I have every intention of purchasing many from you in the time ahead. And I will also remember your offer to be of assistance should I require financing for certain —" I hesitated — "plans."

"Edinburgh is graced by your presence, Your Majesty," he said, and it was one of the few times I'd heard such words spoken with sincerity.

When he had gone, I picked up the little brooch, which sparkled as it caught the light from the window. It was truly a thing of beauty, intricately designed with stones perfectly matched in size and colour. The strange excitement I'd felt earlier upon seeing the array of jewels spread out over the table came over me again. My fingers closed around the brooch and I grasped it tightly, wondering why I had never felt so before.

5

During that cold and snowy February, James and I settled into a routine similar to the one we'd had at Stirling. But there was a subtle new politeness between us, as though we were both more aware of each other and wanted to avoid causing trouble or discord, especially about Henry. Each of us received reports on his progress and care, even regarding inconsequential matters. As we shared them with each other, I arranged a smile on my face, holding my feelings of loss and bitterness at bay, biding my time. An unspoken truce between us had been reached regarding him. But I knew it might very well prove temporary, depending on his response to the next part of my plan. I was adamant that although my child's first birthday had been celebrated without me, under the cold and withering stare of the Countess of Mar, his second would be with his mother by his side.

When my course did not arrive as usual that month, I was nearly ecstatic. "I think I am with child again!" I whispered excitedly to Anna. James had been coming to my bed nightly, so there was every possibility of it. But I had in the past missed a month, only to have the flow resume normally the next, and I knew the change of residence as well as the nearly unbearable recent stresses might have caused the irregularity. So, I refrained from allowing myself to believe it, and sternly warned my women not to speak of it. But when a month later it did not arrive again, I knew it was true, even before the morning the physicians confirmed it.

I was full of giddy triumph. Nothing could have been better to remind James of my importance, of what I could give to him and to Scotland. He would have to be told before that night, for his visits to me would now by necessity be curtailed. After the physicians left I considered how to tell him to best effect: would it be better to do so before the entire court, either in the banquet hall at dinner or the throne room afterward, to impress upon him how the entire country shared in our good fortune? Or should I tell him privately this morning, with affection, to strengthen the intimacy between us? If the latter, should I send a message for him to come to me, or should I just go to him unannounced, as though overcome with the excitement of the news? Or would it be better to wait until he came to me at night, and tell him in the setting of our most intimate time? Or, should I not say anything, and wait until the inevitable court gossip reached his ears?

Finally, I decided on telling him privately, and soon, before the news reached him. I would go to him rather than request his presence, since it would not even give him the few moments to muse over what the news I had for him could be. But just as I was preparing to leave my rooms, the women told me he was on his way to me, accompanied by attendants. He had already heard.

Suddenly I was seized by a desire to tell him alone. I sent my women out, and was standing by myself in the centre of the room when he came in, the others trailing after him. "Send them away," I said irritably, for I had seen by the expressions of the men and women that they already knew. The moment, which had been mine to control, had been taken from me.

He stood a few feet away, looking at me questioningly while the attendants bowed and curtsied, and retreated backwards to the door and out. When the door had closed behind them, I said, "I see you have already heard the news. I am with child. It will arrive in November."

"My satisfaction is great," he said quietly. "Nothing could please me more. I am very happy, Anne." He came close to me, face to face, and took my hand in his, holding it up between us as though sealing an agreement or bond. For a long moment he silently looked down at our joined hands. Then he sighed, and lightly caressed my fingers with his, with equal sensuality and affection. The tiny gesture spoke of his continuing love for me, and my importance in his life. *But how, I wondered, if he truly feels so, has he been able to take my child from me?*

Continuing to look down at my hand, he said, "We will succeed, you and me together, in creating a dynasty, one that will rule a new country. A new Great Britain, composed of the joint kingdoms of England and Scotland. It is what I want for us, and for our children."

There was no need for me to agree, for I'd said as much many times in the past. He was reaffirming our commitment to our mutually agreed joint purpose. He held my hand open, the fingers extended. "Let us have this many children," he said, and then slowly touched each finger. Finishing, he looked into my eyes and smiled. For the first time since the birth of Henry, he looked young again.

I smiled back and said, "That many, at least." *And they will all live with us under one roof,* I thought with great confidence. It was now just a matter of time, and careful planning.

Over the following days I received good wishes and congratulations from many of the court and nobility. Some, finding an opportunity to gain favour, sent gifts. Most impressive was a gold and pearl bracelet, created by the goldsmith Mr Heriot, and delivered in person by him on behalf of the person bestowing it.

"With the compliments and good wishes of the Lord Chancellor," he said.

I hesitated, about to slide the bracelet over my hand onto my wrist. It was an absolute delight, all delicate strands of gold woven together about the pearls, and I could see envy in the eyes of the women leaning in around me for a better look at it. But John Maitland, the Lord Chancellor, hadn't always been a friend to me. He was one of James's oldest and most trusted counsellors, a savvy politician with a wide circle of allies both in Scotland and abroad. I'd at times resented his power among the nobility, in parliament, and with the clergy, and his strong influence over James, who liked and admired him. Others in the nobility had resented him also, and in recent years they had made strides in opposing him and curtailing some of his powers. James had been reluctant to intervene.

The expensive gift was clearly a way of reaching out; he wished to initiate a connection with me, perhaps even an alliance. I looked up into the wise and knowing eyes of Mr Heriot, and asked pointedly, "Are the Lord Chancellor and the Earl of Mar friends?"

"No. They always oppose each other. Each has long distrusted the other's influence with the king."

I slid the bracelet onto my wrist. "Please give the Chancellor my heartiest thanks for his beautiful gift, which I wear with pride. And I would be pleased to receive him, should he wish to visit me."

Anna had been standing nearby, and both witnessed and heard my exchange with Mr Heriot. When he was gone and the women were out of hearing range, she approached me. "Is it wise to dabble in political matters?"

I placed the hand with the bracelet above it on my stomach protectively. "The custom here is for each royal child to have his own household — you were the one who first told me of this. But never will I allow it! I must regain control of my son before the birth of this child. The time is right now to begin. Powerful friends can help me. You know very well how important the Chancellor is. It is he who carries out the running of the country. Aside from the king, he is the most important man in Scotland."

"His motives for anything must be deep and complicated."

"He is no friend of the Earl of Mar," I said pointedly. "The enemy of my enemy is my friend. Besides, James listens to what he says."

The following week the Lord Chancellor came to see me, as I had fully expected he would. I chose to receive him outside in the Privy Garden, where we could speak privately without having my women think it too noticeable, which might then be reported to James. The choice of location itself wasn't unusual, because I had begun walking there every afternoon as soon as the winter had retreated and the snow and ice had vanished.

The day was fine, the sky clear except for occasional drifting clouds, the air still cold but full of the scent of the earth. Clusters of small, budding flowers, the first of the year, appeared at intervals in the rich ground. As the Lord Chancellor appeared in the distance, emerging from the long gallery connecting the palace with the garden, I thought that it was a fitting setting in which to begin to set in motion a new plan.

Whatever attendants had come with him — he was usually accompanied by at least two secretaries, men of importance directing his orders for the administration of the country — had remained in the palace, and he'd come outside alone. The women pointed me out to him, and he approached along a garden path. He walked slowly, but with straighter posture than one usually saw in an older man, especially a veteran of innumerable intense political battles. In the past we'd had only the barest of encounters in crowded settings, and I'd never been able to observe him closely. His manner was solemn, but not grave. His round hat, which he removed as he drew close, was held before him, pressed against his voluminous grey, furtrimmed cloak with both of his gloved hands, as though he were a minister holding his prayer book. When he reached me, I saw that when younger he'd been handsome, before worry lines and creases had taken their toll on his long oval face and well-balanced features. His iron-grey hair was still abundant, and cut close to his head, and his moustache and beard, also grey, were neatly trimmed.

He bowed, lower than I'd thought him capable of. As he stood up, our eyes met, and I saw that his were a light blue; they seemed lively and interesting, still young and full of power despite the ageing face they were set within. They told of someone with a sharp intellect, still capable of holding his own among the vying factions of Scotland, still a force that even the king must reckon with. If anyone could help me recover my son, it would be him.

"Lord Chancellor, we must speak," I said. "Put your hat back on, and draw up the hood of your cloak. I don't want you distracted by the cold. Our conversation may take some time." Beside me, Anna moved, her cloak fluttering. She was the only one of my women who'd accompanied me so far into the garden, almost to the rear wall. I told her to go back with the others. "I am in good company with the chancellor. He will prevent me from losing my step."

"Your Grace," he said, "together we will avoid slipping on any lingering ice, although I doubt there is any. Spring is here, a time of new beginnings." He spoke slowly, his voice pleasant, not loud or forceful. Anna stared at him appraisingly, managing to convey that if she didn't find him trustworthy, she would refuse to leave. Finally, she looked quickly at me, bowed, and backed several feet away before turning and going.

The Lord Chancellor put on his hat, round and cake-like, and made of black velvet, with a large diamond placed above the centre of his forehead. It fit snugly, like a crown, but one for a very specific purpose; the wearer had glory and authority but also worked. He didn't pull up the hood from his cloak. I pushed mine off my head completely; we needed to see each other clearly. The light breeze wasn't too cold, and felt invigorating.

"Your woman protects you," he said approvingly.

"Anna came with me from Denmark. She is my most faithful companion, and my oldest friend in the world."

"New friends can protect you also," he said pointedly.

"Let us walk a bit. May I ask to lean on your arm? Although the path looks clear, it could still be treacherous. And as you know, I am with child."

"For which all of Scotland rejoices." He bowed again, and offered his arm. "You honour me."

I extended my gloved hand from within the folds of my fur cape, and lightly rested it on his forearm. "Let me be frank and direct. You are no friend of the Earl of Mar."

His face showed nothing of his thoughts, though his eyes were keen and focused. He replied, "He is no friend to me. But his enmity is without cause. I never did anything to antagonise him, intentionally or otherwise. Many in Scotland have always resented me. I am neither of the old nobility, nor of the clergy.

I have made my way by my wits and abilities. I have found I threaten those who have not the same, but wish they did."

We began walking down the path alongside the rear wall. I said, "The king appreciates such talent. He values intellect and ability. Even in himself, although he believes firmly that royal birth is at the direction of God. He has shown great talent as a scholar. It is important for him to demonstrate to his subjects why he so relies on his own capacity for thought. He wishes Scotland to see him capable. That God was not mistaken in making him a king."

"As perhaps he was in making his mother a queen?"

It was shocking to hear it finally said outright. No one else had ever dared say so to me. Still, I needed to be careful. "God does not make mistakes, my Lord Chancellor. Sometimes his ways are mysterious. But I appreciate your frankness."

He said, "We must never forget it was those unfortunate parents who brought us such an excellent king, who we appreciate all the more for his contrast with them. The ways of God certainly are mysterious. Indeed, he does not make mistakes. It is us humans who make them." He paused, then added drily, "The parents of the king made great ones. Especially his mother."

By taking such a chance in his honesty, he was showing me we could trust each other. He had decided — correctly — that I wouldn't repeat his remarks to James. He was someone I could speak my mind with, and whom I could learn from.

We walked a few steps in silence, flanked by the newly budded flowers. The sad legacy of James's parents, two people I'd never met, felt so much stronger at Holyrood than at Stirling, or any of our other residences. They must have walked in this same privy garden, together at first, but then alone, as they'd schemed against each other. It may have been on this same path that Mary Stuart had plotted Lord Darnley's destruction.

"Did you know them?" I asked. "The king's parents?" The Lord Chancellor was old enough to have met them. I knew from his earlier remark that it was unlikely that whatever he had to say would be flattering. But it would be interesting to hear it without the religious sourness and distortion the Countess of Mar had expressed.

"I was at the very beginning of my career, newly returned from Europe. I never had cause to speak to either. But I did watch them. It was impossible not to, for anyone who had anything to do with the court. Both were rather dazzling, not only in their physical attractiveness, but their charm. Her especially. She had beauty enough, but there was an air about her, a presence, that drew all eyes towards her. It is one of those things some people just have. As if they know they are special, and make others believe it too. Those around them either accept it, and flow towards them, or fear the power of it, and respond with suspicion. And so it went with her in Scotland: the Catholics adored her, but the Calvinists responded with great suspicion, especially the clergy. You must remember the reformed faith was still young here — everywhere, at that time — and the clergy were jealous of their new power. We spoke before of mistakes. I believe it was Mary Stuart's greatest mistake not to have converted to Calvinism."

I hadn't expected so long and detailed an answer, although given his statesmanship, and his need to often explain his policies, perhaps I should have. What he was saying was fascinating, and I wanted to know more. "Religious belief is not so easily discarded," I said.

"For her it was politics. She wanted the English throne. The strength of her claim lay in her Catholicism. Elizabeth's claim was — is — rooted in the acceptance of the validity of her parents' marriage, which caused the English break from Rome. For the Catholics, she was, and still is, a bastard. Queen Mary thought the Catholic support would bring her that throne. She was determined to get it. That type of person, one who from birth has believed in their own specialness, will stop at nothing to get what they want. Those who are of royal birth further believe God himself has decreed their specialness. They use it to absolve themselves of poor behaviour. It is reported that Mary Stuart was heard to say it was her God-given right to destroy her enemies. She failed to see how self-serving such a way of thinking could become, and it led her into mistakes, some well-known, others only inferred. It was clear, for instance, that she came to believe Lord Darnley was an enemy. And she made many, many others, albeit with less drastic results."

He stopped walking; since I was leaning on his arm, I did also. He turned to me, looking down at my face. He said, "King James has also made mistakes. Few, very few. But one of them is the choice of the Earl of Mar as guardian of the prince."

He was slightly taller than me, but in that moment, he seemed to tower above me, a reflection of his vastly superior intellectual ability, which he'd just so impressively demonstrated. He had not rambled, but carefully arranged his words to make a powerful point. It was no wonder he had lasted so long at the centre of Scottish politics.

"Why have you not advised him differently?"

"I have. But the king must often find a way among many differing opinions. He has always agreed with me on the two main issues of policy — that Scotland must reach accords internally with the clergy, and externally, with England. But in other areas, he sometimes listens more to others. He is at times especially inclined to want to please the old nobility. The Earl of Mar is preeminent among them. I will be frank, Your Majesty. I, and a number of lords, would like to see the prince maintained differently."

It was exactly what I wanted to hear, and more: that other lords already wanted what I did was something I hadn't dared to hope for. I had never doubted I would succeed in having Henry returned to my care, but I'd thought it would be a long and difficult struggle to accomplish. But now it suddenly seemed that it might be achieved in only a matter of weeks. "Lord Chancellor, above all else, that is what I want. I would be forever grateful for your assistance."

"It would require the support of a number of powerful lords. Members of Parliament, as well as others who advise the king. It is the way of things in Scotland, where we have lords with great power."

"What of the clergy? Would it help to win their support?"

He shook his head. "Better to avoid them if possible. The king already resents their attempts to interfere with his personal life. Their inclusion might strengthen his resolve to steer his own path. I think it best not to let this issue divide along religious lines. We will need to draw Calvinist and Catholic lords alike to our side. Which brings me to a question, which I trust I will not cause offence by asking. But I must do so, to be able to set our course best."

"Ask," I said confidently.

"There are those who doubt your commitment to Calvinism. Are you a Catholic?"

"No. Here in Scotland I conform to the religion of my husband, and am satisfied to do so. I would hope others remember I was raised Lutheran, in Denmark. In time, should things go as I hope, there will be another change for me, to the reformed ways of the Church of England. Anglican, I believe they call it there. For the king also. Although as a child he was taught a strict Calvinism, his education taught him broader views of life."

There was a slight pause before he said, "He also, at a very young age, understood the English throne was within his grasp. Catholicism failed to bring it to his mother."

For the first time in our conversation, I disliked what he was suggesting. "He is not an opportunist. One of his ambitions is to bring peace to Europe, which would involve religious harmony and respect. He sets an example in his own behaviour. So he tolerates the Catholics, as do I. But I am not one." Anna's face flickered through my thoughts. I considered telling him that some very close to me had leanings that way, but I decided against it. Even should she actually convert, or if she had already, I would not allow it to influence me.

He bowed a little, lowering his eyes in deference. "As I said, Your Majesty, the king has made very few mistakes, and his handling of the religious divisions has been wise. He is always on guard against those who would use them to manipulate him. So must you be. I needed reassurance that you understood this before we embark on your endeavour."

"And have I reassured you?"

"Yes."

We resumed walking. Apparently, my responses had satisfied him, and the disapproval I had shown over his suggestion of James's opportunism hadn't discouraged or offended him. He said, "In Scotland it is traditional for the prince to have his own household, away from his parents. This is different in Denmark, and I know even without your saying so you would have it the way it is there."

With determination, I replied, "I would. And I am going to have it so."

"I recommend we proceed in two steps, which will be easier to accomplish separately. First, we remove the prince from the Earl of Mar. Second, we bring him back to your household. The king has indicated he wishes to remain much in Edinburgh in the future. We should seek to have the prince moved into his own household in Edinburgh Castle, with a different guardian. I understand you would prefer to have him with you at Holyrood Palace, but if we press the king too hard all at once it decreases the possibility of our success. This way would be less of a change, still allowing him to adhere to the tradition of Scottish princes having their own households. It would also bring the prince very close to you, permanently; you could see him every day. And it would remove him from the influence of the Earl and Countess of Mar."

The wisdom of the plan was easy to see. Edinburgh Castle was little more than a mile away from Holyrood Palace, at the other end of the city. It was perched on a rocky hill the way Stirling Castle was, and was just as much a fortress. Henry could be well protected there, which should satisfy James's concern on that count. It could also appeal to him to have his son more visible to the city, fitting with his plans for us to reside more permanently there. "I like this plan," I said. "Once established in the city, it shouldn't be too difficult to have the prince moved over here."

"Or you could move to the castle. The king's desire is to remain in Edinburgh, but not necessarily at Holyrood Palace."

Again, I was deeply impressed by the way he had thought things through. "I understand, Lord Chancellor, how you have maintained your position for so long, and so successfully. This is an extremely good plan! But how do we remove the Earl of

Mar? To have him — and his mother — continue in their same roles here in Edinburgh would be to leave the situation nearly as unacceptable to me as it is now."

"The king would not bring him to Edinburgh, in so important a position. It would be unbalancing for him to have so powerful an earl, even one that he trusts, right here in the city. Remember, the king is a very savvy politician, despite his relative youth. Every move is calculated and considered and weighed in advance. I can suggest to him that he choose someone less identified with the Calvinists, someone more moderate and less well known."

"Someone who will not object so much when the position is no longer needed."

The chancellor stopped walking and looked at me, an appreciative half smile on his face. "I see, Your Grace, that you would make a fine politician yourself. You look ahead." His eyebrows drew together thoughtfully. "There are those who would be interested in forming a party around you, were your talents understood."

No one had ever suggested it to me before. I had avoided politics, not only because I had not felt competent to engage in the complicated Scottish struggles and factions, but also from a lack of interest. I had never wanted to expand the power I had as queen, for I'd had no need to do so. But the events of the past few months had changed things. James might have thought more deeply over how I would respond to being separated from Henry if he'd felt my power more equal to his own. He might not even have considered it at all.

I looked up at the sky. All around me the crisp spring air seemed to be pulsing with life. The child within me was still too young to be felt directly — there was nothing yet except the nausea every morning — but at that moment I was intensely aware of his or her presence. I would do whatever I could to become more powerful to provide protection, even from the misguided actions of his or her own father. Never again would a child of mine be taken from me.

"Such a position interests me," I replied strongly. "In these modern times we have seen that a queen can wield as much power as a king, and as effectively. Elizabeth has been one of England's greatest rulers. She failed in one respect only, in not producing an heir — which I have already done. I can show myself to be as wise as her. Scotland will see that not only is this queen very different from the last one, but also that the king is very different from his father. Together we will show that we can overcome differences, where his parents could not."

The chancellor eyed me appraisingly, and was quick to utter a warning: "The king may initially resist your growing power."

"But I believe he will eventually come to see the benefit of it. James wishes to bring harmony to Europe, to show that the powerful can work together. What better way to begin than to demonstrate it within his own marriage?"

The chancellor reached up and adjusted his round hat, shifting it slightly on the crown of his head. Although earlier it had looked formal and impressive, almost regal, it now looked like part of the attire of a successful Scottish burgher or merchant, one who had just concluded the sale of an important piece of merchandise. "But we mustn't move too quickly," he said cautiously. "First, I need time to consult the lords who have already expressed dissatisfaction with the prince's current household, and to draw others into our party. And it would be better for more time to pass between you and the king, so he feels you have accepted the guardianship of the Earl of Mar. It will be some weeks before we can approach him. The first step, of course, once the pieces are in place, should be for you to make the request of him for a change. If he agrees, other measures would be avoided. But if not, we then proceed with them."

It was disappointing not to be able to move quicker, but I could stand the absence of my child a little longer, so long as in the end he was brought back to me. "My Lord Chancellor, with confidence I am guided by you in this matter."

He gently withdrew his forearm from beneath my hand, stepped backward, and bowed. "Your Grace should find that your confidence has not been misplaced." As he stood up, he smiled. I now saw on his face an expression of excitement. There were such men who were driven by the thrill of a struggle, of challenges to their wits and intellect, and he was one of them. But for me the possibility of more power was still secondary to the return of my child.

He backed away a few steps, then turned and left. There was a lively rhythm to his footsteps as he moved across the garden path, suggesting he was leaving much satisfied.

That night, after supper, it had been planned for the court to hear a new ballad by one of the Edinburgh poets who had sought our patronage. But instead, I called for music, announcing, "We will dance the Almain!"

There was applause from the courtiers and exclamations of approval, for we had not danced much since coming to Holyrood. I looked at James and smiled. I didn't often request that he dance, knowing that he didn't like it, and was at times awkward at it. But I'd deliberately chosen the Almain because it was slow and stately, one of the easier dances, and the music was rhythmic and soothing.

The musicians started playing. Without comment, James took my hand and helped me to my feet, and led me down amidst the courtiers who had already formed pairs to follow us. The music paused and then started again, more loudly, the signal to begin. Together, in perfect harmony, we began the formal pattern of steps and little kicks and turnings. It was just what I'd wanted; as we led everyone gracefully across the floor, our dancing felt the perfect symbol of our marriage, one of unity and equality.

James danced well, for not having had any recent practice. Later, as my women helped me prepare for bed, they all spoke of how fine we had looked together. "The king cannot come to my bed now that I am with child," I replied. "During these months it is important for us to maintain intimacy in other ways. Although I am a queen, I am still a wife and mother."

"The English queen is neither," one of them said, and there was quiet laughter from the others.

I always frowned upon any negative discussion of Elizabeth, and now said, "That queen has been a great leader of her nation."

Behind me, I heard Anna's clear voice say, "She feared both marriage and motherhood. She saw her mother destroyed by her father, and two of her stepmothers died in childbirth."

"Jane Seymour and Catherine Parr," one of the women said knowingly.

"And she saw how marriage destroyed her sister's popularity," added another. "Poor Mary Tudor."

I remembered the sad story of Elizabeth's older sister, and her desperate and unfulfilled desire to have a child. I said, "Queen Mary Tudor's life and reign would have turned out differently if she'd successfully given birth. Especially to a son." At once, I felt the loss and sadness I always did when I thought of Henry. But for the first time it wasn't as sharp and biting as it had been before.

"Don't be so sure Queen Mary Tudor would have been happy had she borne a child," Anna said. "Men aren't used to women having power. They don't like women's ability to rule *and* produce a child." Warningly, she added, "Despite whatever Chancellor Maitland has been telling you."

I turned to face her. "Leave us!" I ordered the other women, who immediately retreated to the outer room. When the door had closed behind them, I told Anna, "Do not criticise me in front of the women again! You know not to do that — what is wrong with you?"

"I am sorry," she said quietly, then curtsied low before me.

"I want my child back, Anna! And I'm going to do whatever I can to ensure none is ever taken from me again." I climbed into my empty bed, regretting that James would not be joining me in it, but comforted by the thought of the child within me.

6

It wasn't until the end of May that I received word from the chancellor that everything was in order for me to approach James. Much had been done in preparation during the intervening weeks since we'd had our first discussion in the privy garden, and members of James's council were ready to support the changes. I had also had a meeting with Mr Heriot and arranged to have money available should I need to encourage other lords whose political interests might not be sufficient. The time was right for me to begin.

We were at Linlithgow Palace, where we'd moved at the beginning of the month. The change had suited me, for I'd always liked the pale-coloured stone palace in its setting of rolling, gentle lawns on the banks of Linlithgow Loch. It had been built as a pleasure palace, unlike Stirling Castle, which was a fortress, and Holyrood Palace with its ancient abbey connection. Four ranges of elegant rooms reached by numerous winding staircases surrounded a square courtyard, in the centre of which was an ornately carved fountain. Large windows were everywhere, in both the courtyard and outer walls, and the many chimneys topping each range told of the comfort of the rooms within, no matter the season.

I liked the palace even better now since it was closer to Henry at Stirling Castle, and also because it wasn't so steeped in the sad history of James's parents. Mary Stuart had been born there, but had soon gone to Stirling Castle. When she'd returned from France, she had resided there but little. Our change of residence felt to be a removal from her shadow, and promised a better outcome to the problems of my marriage.

The serenity of the loch and continual flow of the fountain were calming, and might be conducive to James's coming to feel there would be no danger in Henry's removal to Edinburgh Castle, and eventually into my care.

The royal apartments were on the second floor, overlooking the courtyard. The attendants and courtiers occupied the floors above. The walls were covered with rich tapestries and the rooms were filled with fine furniture. My rooms and James's were further apart than at Holyrood, but even so it felt as if we were closer, in more of a home. The palace had the feeling of one large mansion, compact, with everything designed to fit together, instead of rambling like our other residences. It also felt very far away from Edinburgh, not merely fifteen miles, despite the daily flow of visitors and messengers and couriers from the city.

During our first weeks there James appeared calmer. His gestures and walk, always fast and at times awkward, seemed smoother. He rode every day, rowed on the loch, and hunted, and when not attending to state matters spent more time with me and the court, instead of closeted away with his books and studies. He appeared satisfied and happy. It wasn't only our being at Linlithgow; he was enjoying other success. Remarks by important councillors were reported back to me, indicating his policies were finally bearing fruit, and he had achieved a balance between the clergy and the Catholic earls. For this accomplishment, he had the admiration of much of Europe, and especially his cousin Elizabeth. It was whispered that, although still refusing to confirm the succession, she'd been overheard saying, "Who better to succeed me, than a king?" I was also told that he was greatly pleased with his domestic life, delighted that he would soon have another child.

The morning of the day I chose to request the dismissal of the Earl of Mar and the transfer of Henry to Edinburgh Castle, I arose full of confidence, sure of my success. I would wait until midday, right after dinner, when James was usually most agreeable, the morning's work behind him, and I would accompany him back to his rooms and speak to him privately.

I experienced my first feelings of doubt as I was about to leave my bedroom for dinner. What if he refused? Was I fully prepared to confront him, and take more drastic steps? Outside my window the loch looked serene in the clear May sunlight, an unbroken surface of blue surrounded by green shores. My dress was of green satin, and I hoped it would carry some of the calm of the landscape over to me. I decided that if I became agitated, I would imagine the serenity of the loch and its setting. I would also think of the heart-shaped gold and ruby brooch that James had given me, and which I now wore prominently on my breast. He might see it, and remember the feelings that had prompted the gift after our reconciliation at Holyrood.

Emboldened, I led my women into the adjacent room which ran nearly the full northern side of the palace, where the members of my household gathered to follow me into the Great Hall. As usual they separated for me to pass, all bowing as I did. But today it felt as if they were observing me with special interest. I was seized by concern that somehow, they all knew of my intention to speak to James about Henry, and were eagerly anticipating a battle the way they would a joust or a tournament. But that was impossible, for I'd spoken to no one of my plan, not even Anna. Quickly, I thought of the loch and breathed deeply. My concerns were only imaginings, and I pushed them away.

We turned a corner, passing the upper kitchen where foods were held prior to being served. Fortunately, the morning nausea I'd had after first becoming with child had stopped, and the aromas of the waiting dishes didn't provoke it. But they did remind me of my condition, and the unusual moods I'd been warned it might cause. I'd had none while carrying Henry, but I'd been told each time could vary from the one before, especially if the child was a different sex. My moods could be because I was carrying a girl. If so, it would be vitally important that I raise her myself; to have her taken from me might be even more painful than Henry's removal, my having seen my own reflection in her, as mothers sometimes did with daughters. The thought steadied my resolve to win back the care of my son. Too much time had already passed without him.

But as I entered the vast Great Hall, I suddenly felt overwhelmed by its size, dwarfed by its lofty reaches, and diminished by the crowd from James's household already there, waiting to take their places. At the far end James stood, talking with a small group of courtiers. *You're being ridiculous*, I told myself sternly. *You are a queen, and these are all your subjects. You have nothing to fear here; it is all from the disruption of your humours from the child you carry.* I thought of the loch again, and once more it proved calming, although not as much as previously.

Slowly, I moved through the crowded hall. All the members of James's household bowed and curtsied, while behind me those from mine broke away and waited near their places at the two long tables. By the time I reached the end, I was alone. James left those he'd been talking with, who went to find their places, as ushers stepped forward and formally led me to my seat. As they did, the three great fireplace bays, unused now it was late spring, suddenly appeared to represent three different choices. It occurred to me that although the clergy might speak to us of fate and predestination, our lives seemed directed by choices we made ourselves.

"Is something troubling you, Anne?" James startled me by asking, and I turned to find him beside me, watching me closely. His blue eyes were wider than usual, and for the first time in months I noticed the depth to them, and their attractiveness. It wasn't often that I thought of him as handsome, although I had always found him appealing, but today I did. There was a robust and vital quality about him I hadn't noticed the entire winter. *What would happen*, I wondered, *if he refused my request, and the breach between us opened again, and widened? Would the love between us be lost forever?* And it seemed a terrible thing that the cause would be a child. But that would not happen. I had only to speak to him a little later and all would be fine.

"Nothing at all," I said, wondering if he'd noticed the brooch and remembered its significance.

We went through the formalities of the starting of dinner, the trumpet blasts and the prayers, and the servants brought the first course. I thought of the conversation with James that was to follow, and my appetite faded, but I knew I needed to fortify myself, so I partook of each dish, including the pottage, which I normally refused. James noticed my appetite. He said, with a touch of amusement, "The child will be of great strength." He then gestured for the waiting server, who came forward and filled my silver cup with wine, which I immediately drank deeply of.

I ate some of nearly everything served: pies, filled with chickens, capons, ducks and pigeons, with stuffing full of hard-boiled eggs, and plums, everything seasoned with saffron and honey; roast venison and wild boar; sturgeon; cheeses, sweet tarts and custards and candied and preserved fruits. When the final course was finished, I dipped my fingers in the presented bowl of water, and dried them on my white linen napkin. James and I stood in unison, and everyone else in the crowded hall did the same. From both sides, our attendants gathered around us. "Anne," James said, bowing slightly and removing his tall hat, and I curtsied in response. It was time to tell him I wished to speak with him, alone. But no words would pass my lips. I stood and watched as he left through the nearby door, his attendants trailing after him.

"Some of the women think you might enjoy a walk outside," Anna offered. "Since the day is so fine."

It would be so easy to go down to the loch and laugh with them in the sunlight, and listen to their idle tales, so easy to forget about ever having met with Chancellor Maitland, and instead merely adjust myself to Henry having his own household at Stirling. James and I were so harmonious now; it would surely be beneficial to continue it. There would be no loss of dignity for me as queen, no diminishment in my position, for it was traditional for royal children to be so maintained in Scotland. Why not just go down to the loch with my women and leave things alone with James?

And then I thought of the new child within me, and knew I could not. I was the daughter of a king, and not inclined to give up something of such importance to me. "No," I replied. "I have a matter I must discuss with the king." All the diners had by now left, and my words seemed to echo through the hall.

I told the women they should go to the loch, and I would join them later. Anna alone I kept with me, although we didn't speak as we left the hall and passed through the chapel, on the way to James's rooms. Tension caused my temples to throb, and my heart to feel as though it were pounding. Attempting to think of the loch or my brooch to calm myself was useless, and in the midst of the chapel I thought I should try to pray, even to the Catholic Mary, who as a mother might respond. Anna might know of a prayer to her, but even in my agitation I knew I might be overheard if I asked her. And before the words of any Calvinist prayer could form in my mind, we were at the door to James's rooms. Deftly, Anna stepped in front of me and opened it. As we stepped inside the crowded room, everyone turned to me and bowed or curtsied. I saw at once that James wasn't there, so I told the guards I wished to see him. One of them motioned to a nearby servant, who hurried through the crowd into the inner bedroom.

A moment later James appeared in the anteroom. He had taken off his hat, and looked less formidable than at dinner. "Away," he said, and all of his attendants left, the guards drawing the doors shut behind them as they stepped out. I caught sight of Anna's worried face as she turned to look back at me, the doors closing behind her.

With no one but us left, the large room looked different, being sparsely furnished with only chairs and benches. It was the only one in the royal apartments with no tapestries, and the stone walls had been painted a stark white. The midday light poured in through the large windows, but the room felt ruthlessly empty and neutral, absent of any cheerfulness or welcome.

James pulled a chair forward, and motioned for me to sit. I did, and he pulled up another and sat before me. "And so?" he asked.

His hair was slightly dishevelled from when he'd removed his hat, and the sight of it was reassuring and familiar. Better to begin at once, before my courage failed. "I want to speak with you about our son."

He looked away from me, to the floor; he'd clearly guessed what was coming.

"For three months I have done my best to reconcile myself to the arrangement you have felt necessary, but it is no easier for me now than it was in February," I said. "I find the separation from the prince unbearable. It is as though a part of myself has been torn away, leaving in its place an emptiness that I have been unable to fill. I have tried, James. Surely you have seen that."

His eyes turned up to my face, and he drew a slight breath as though preparing to say something. I was certain there was sympathy in his expression, that he not only recognised the depth of my feelings, but that they stirred his own. So far, I'd succeeded, and my hopes took a great leap forward.

With more confidence, I continued, "Do not make me remain in this state of separation from my child. Could you not allow the creation of a household for him at Edinburgh Castle? For then, when we are at Holyrood, I could see him every day. You would find such an arrangement satisfactory, would you not? The castle is one of the strongest in Scotland."

Abruptly his head tilted forward, his eyes looking again at the floor. My hopes began to plummet. Around us, the room felt intolerably vacant, as void of human feeling as of furnishings and décor. But I'd already said too much to stop, and had no choice but to go on, trying to keep any hint of desperation from my voice.

"Do not doubt the great love I have for you, and my respect for your wisdom. Never have I opposed you in anything, great or small, either in our life together or in matters of state."

Still, he said nothing; his sitting so quietly was unnerving.

"James, have you ever had cause for complaint with me, not only as a wife, but as a queen? Haven't I supported all your policies, and kept strong the friendship between you and my brother the Danish king?"

Finally, he answered, but still with his face averted. "You know I have no complaint. You have been exemplary as both a wife and a queen. I would have you now do the same as a mother."

His voice sounded thin and brittle, as though he were withholding much that he might have said. Was there a rebuke in his words? The suggestion that if I did not follow his wishes, I would be inadequate? Resentment tore at me. I was a queen, and shouldn't be condescended to. The only difference in our stations was that he'd been born to reign. Strongly, I exclaimed, "I can do that best by having my child with me! It is both reasonable and natural for a mother to be expected to take the best care of her child. And who better to care for a prince than a queen?"

He jumped up, as though some released mechanism had caused him to spring to his feet. His words were sharp and low, delivered with the speed of an arrow: "This is a prince of a particularly factious and quarrelsome people. He needs the protection of a strong and competent earl. Such is the Earl of Mar."

Weeks ago, the chancellor, anticipating James's argument, had given me the words which I now threw back at him: "The Earl of Mar is neither of your own house of Stuart, nor of such accomplished ability to be so entrusted. Surely you can do better for our only child! Remove Henry to Edinburgh Castle, and choose another guardian better deserving. Or best, place him in the care of his own mother!"

James strode to the window and leaned on the stone wall beside it, looking out. Against the sunlight only his silhouette was visible. "No," he said harshly.

Tears of disappointment and frustration began to flow from my eyes. With bitterness, I said, "And so am I rewarded for my loyalty and love! The wife of the poorest peasant in Scotland would be better treated by her husband!"

"You are the Queen of Scotland, madam!" he shouted, standing away from the wall, his shape against the sunlit window seeming to tremble with the words.

Startled, I sobbed loudly, not out of fear, but out of despair at his commitment to the course he had set.

He quickly came forward so I could see him clearly. "Anne," he said urgently, but in a steady tone, "do not disbelieve that I suffer to see you so unhappy. I understand your good intentions, and I respect your attempts to dissuade me from a decision you believe is wrong. But I am not wrong. I have enemies, both here in this kingdom and abroad. Balancing these Scottish factions has tested me to the very limit of my abilities, which are prodigious beyond what God gives even to kings. Maintaining that balance among the factions requires constant vigilance. Should one of them begin to dominate, they would seek to use Henry for their own purposes. It would require the undivided attention of one with the utmost abilities to prevent it."

"Remember, I am the daughter of a king!" I said forcefully. "Descended from those who took the Danish crown, and held it. I have abilities sufficient to protect what is mine!"

He shook his head. "You would not be able to prevent our child from being used against me as I was used against my mother."

"Never would I let that happen," I replied vehemently.

"I even question my own ability to prevent it! But I have the advantage of having lived among the Scots all my life, and I have observed and studied them. You have not lived here so long. Nor did my mother. She had not the understanding of her opponents, or her allies. France, where she grew up, is very different from Scotland. So is Denmark."

"I am not Mary Stuart!" I cried.

Very slowly and determinedly, he said, "And I am not my father." Finishing, he became extremely still, as though he barely breathed. He stared past me, somewhere into the blank and empty room.

In the pause that followed, I remembered what the chancellor had told me to say. I wiped the tears from my face. "Can you at least seek the advice of your council?"

"No."

"There may be those more skilled at persuasion than I am."

"No."

"The council —"

"The council," he interrupted, "does not rule here, any more than does the clergy. I am king. I have no peer to advise me in a matter such as this. I have only myself, and my own experience. In that, the loyalty of the family of the Earl of Mar has shown itself. Henry is to stay with them, at Stirling."

I saw it was useless for me to try further to deter or shake him. I was grappling with his sense of personal security and fears, and in the end, they would be stronger than his love for me. The more I argued and pleaded, the more resolved he would become. He would not do what I wanted -- not of his own choice.

Very slowly, with as much dignity as possible, I stood up. "Then there is nothing more for us to discuss," I said with perfect calm.

He blinked, appearing surprised I wouldn't continue the argument. "I am happy to see you have become so reasonable," he said. Then he changed the subject. "I was about to go rowing on the loch. Would you care to join me?"

But the thought of the loch no longer produced the calm in me it had earlier. "Perhaps later," I said. Then I curtsied deeply, and left the room at the far end, opposite where I'd entered. No guards had been posted there, and I pushed the door open myself, and shut it behind me. As I did, I heard the commotion of the courtiers all returning to the empty room behind me.

The two rooms I passed through on the way to my own were empty — our private dining room and my own anteroom. There, voices outside drew me to a window, and I looked out into the courtyard below. James was crossing it, surrounded by his attendants, on their way to the loch. He passed and went out the entrance, the others trailing after him, the sounds of their lively chatter diminishing until the last of them had gone. Then there was only the elaborately carved fountain, its water flowing, as indifferent to the silence and emptiness as it had been to the crowd of cheerful courtiers.

The door I'd entered through began to open, interrupting the silence. It was rare that I was alone, and I wasn't used to it.

It was Anna. "You shouldn't be unattended," she said.

"I can be alone, at times," I replied. "And I'm not really alone. I am with child."

She joined me at the window. "All the more reason for you not to be left unattended. I thought you'd gone with the king to the loch."

"We've gone our separate ways."

"You could join him again," she suggested.

"Perhaps, I might." Outside, I could hear the flow of the fountain in the otherwise silent courtyard. "But not now. Now, I need to write a letter. Could you bring me paper and pen?"

She went to get them, and I moved towards my bedroom, already beginning to mentally compose the letter I would send to Chancellor Maitland. A second letter would likely be necessary, to Mr Heriot, telling him I would need more money.

As I entered the bedroom, I thought sadly of how differently I felt from when I had left it, a short while ago before dinner. Since then I had walked all the way through all four ranges of the palace, and arrived back where I had started. But nothing was the same, because things had changed between James and myself forever. When Anna came with the paper and pen, I would tell her I wouldn't be going to the loch, as planned. Nor would I go to the window to look out at it, for I was sure that the sight of its still waters, which I'd previously found so calming, would now only look cold and unmoving.

Calmly, my fingers found their way to the heart-shaped brooch, and unpinned it. Then I hurled it away, across the room.

7

A few days later, James came to my bedroom early in the morning and said, "Why don't you visit Stirling Castle when I go to Falkland Palace tomorrow? You could spend time with Henry, and I could join you there when I finish at Falkland."

Despite having sent everyone from the room the day of our argument, some in the corridor had overheard it. Since then I had carefully shown no sign of any disagreement or tension between us, but there had been rumours. If I'd heard them, so had James, and I was sure his suggesting I go to Stirling Castle was motivated more by his wanting to display a sign of accord between me and the Earl of Mar, than from sympathy for my missing my child. I smiled pleasantly and said, "No."

"After the impressive display of your feelings of loss, I would expect you would welcome the opportunity."

"I don't wish to be thought to honour the wedding of the kin of that dreadful woman." The Countess of Mar had filled Henry's household with her relatives. She had recently arranged the marriage of one to a prominent lord, and it was to take place in a few days. "Besides that, I have not felt so well these past few days."

He said nothing else on the matter. We chatted about trivial things for a few minutes, and he left. "That won't be the end of it," Anna warned.

"I'm staying here," I answered. Indeed, it was important I did. A company of armed men, quietly being assembled by friends of Chancellor Maitland and financed through Mr Heriot, would arrive while James was away. They would accompany me to Stirling Castle, where they would help me take charge of my son and bring him to Edinburgh Castle. By the time James found out, it would be done. No doubt he would be angry, but I had decided it was necessary even before the door had closed behind me on the afternoon of my unsuccessful attempts to convince him. Any lingering hesitation had vanished as I'd watched him from the window, blithely crossing the courtyard for an afternoon of rowing. The conversation for me had been devastating, forcing me to recognise that the perfect accord I'd thought existed between us was an illusion. It was something I'd first seen at Holyrood when he'd told me the prince had been removed from my care, but I'd somehow avoided fully acknowledging it. Now, that avoidance was no longer possible. I still loved him, and believed he loved me, but it would be necessary for new rights and boundaries to be defined. I would not be condescended to. He would need to understand I was a queen who would not be disregarded so easily. And so I had gone about my plans, carefully timed for when he would be on progress, which I would not accompany him on because the incessant travel would not be wise in my condition.

Anna was right, and in little more than an hour, a message arrived from him. He had consulted with my physicians, all of whom felt that not only was my health fine for the fifteen-mile coach ride to Stirling Castle, but that I would benefit from the excursion. Once there, I need not attend the wedding if I chose not to.

I started to give a reply restating that I would not go, but stopped. Instead, I said I would need one extra day to prepare, as it was a last-minute change of plans. But by all means, he should leave as scheduled. I asked if he could be so gracious as to inform the Earl of Mar that I would be arriving and to have my apartments readied. Meanwhile, I gave orders for my household to prepare for the move.

The next morning, I accompanied him with my women to the palace gatehouse, where he kissed me goodbye before mounting his horse and riding off with his entire household. I remained there until not only James was out of sight, but the last of the long line of riders and coaches and baggage wagons were gone. Back inside, in the centre of the courtyard right beside the steadily flowing fountain, I said loudly, for not only my women but anyone else at the windows above to hear, "I find I'm not feeling so well today. I must return to my rooms to lie down."

In the morning, as soon as Anna pulled back the bed drapes, I said, "I am sick."

She eyed me questioningly. "You look quite well to me, Your Grace."

"I am sick," I repeated. "The trip to Stirling Castle must be cancelled. Please have the household unpack, and ask someone to send a message to the Earl of Mar. I'll write one to James myself." I thought for a moment. "Better yet, you write it. Say that I'm too sick to do so myself."

"You look well enough. I'll write that you *say* you are too sick to do it."

Our eyes met, and I saw the disapproval in hers. But there had been other times when I'd seen much more of it. I leaned back on my pillows. "You can also say I haven't got out of bed today."

I would have preferred the messages to go slowly, but I had to be convincing, so the usual fast riders were sent. By late morning we received word that the earl, concerned by my illness, was on his way to visit me.

"Close the gates!" I ordered. "Do not let him even enter the courtyard!"

"Your Grace," Anna said severely, "the king would be horrified should you treat his friend so. It is a dangerous game you are playing, and you will defeat yourself behaving so. When he arrives, you must receive him immediately."

"I am queen, not you!" I shouted. "It is not for you to tell me what to do. You forget yourself!"

The other women retreated to the furthest reaches of the bedroom, but Anna neither cowered nor flinched. "It is you who forget yourself," she said reproachfully. "Never have I seen you so foolish. You will bring yourself to grief, along with your husband and son."

Suddenly I felt a nameless fear. I buried my face in my hands and whispered, "You don't know what it is to be a mother, and to have your child removed from you."

"It is true I do not," I heard her say. "But that is irrelevant. Many women are mothers, but few are queens. It is different for you; you cannot simply follow the dictates of your heart. The earl as well as the king would be terribly offended if you turned him away."

I dropped my hands from my face. "He thinks to make a show of great concern for me by this visit. I'm not going to be used to his advantage."

"Then simply refuse to see him. But you must allow him to enter the palace."

I grasped the bed curtain and yanked it closed between us. Then I lay back down and pressed the pillows to my ears to drown out anything more she might have to say.

The Earl of Mar arrived mid-afternoon, but got no further than the upper room where my household gathered; I told the women to tell him I was too sick to receive him. Several hours later, he departed, returning to Stirling Castle. Anna told me, "He left before supper. The grooms heard him grumbling he wouldn't stay where he was so clearly unwelcome."

"I merely said I wasn't able to have company."

"Everyone here knew you didn't want to see him." She gestured to the women across the room. "They overheard you this morning, and they talk. Your household does what they think pleases you. They treated him rudely."

"Well, I didn't tell them to." But I turned away so she couldn't see me smile.

The next morning, I received a message from James enquiring as to the state of my health. I would have liked for Anna to reply for me, but I knew she was still angry about my pretence, and might refuse outright. I didn't want to have to contend with such a challenge. Her position with me was twofold, since she was both a friend and a subordinate. She was invaluable to me, yet could become stubborn in ways I didn't appreciate. But there was nothing to prevent her packing up and returning to Denmark if she so desired, and no matter how irritated I became with her, I knew I needed to make sure that never happened. She was my only trusted confidante, and my life in Scotland would be unbearable without her. I wondered if she knew there were times when I resented her independence, having neither husband nor children nor subjects to be accountable to. As I wrote the reply to James — lightly, not pressing hard with the pen, as though I had barely the strength to write — I thought that Anna may very well have chosen the better life, being unencumbered by a husband. Queen Elizabeth would surely agree.

The message said that I was improving, but slowly, and would likely be in my bed for another week. For James to think me bedridden would be convenient. Within two or three days' time, the band of armed men would arrive for my expedition to Stirling. I would know exactly when, when I heard again from the Lord Chancellor.

That news arrived late the same day with a courier from Mr Heriot in Edinburgh, bearing a trinket for my approval. But once in my presence the man whispered the name of the chancellor, and I knew he wasn't from the goldsmith, and the box he was holding would be empty. I waved my women away, saying it was a gift being prepared for the king and must be kept secret.

We hovered together over the box while he delivered his message: the plan was set for three days hence. I was to rise during the night and announce that I would go to Stirling to see the prince immediately, and with as few attendants as possible, leaving most of my household asleep. Halfway there, my coach would be joined by twenty-five men, who would accompany me the rest of the way. So as not to attract attention, three other groups of twenty-five would assemble separately and converge in the town below the castle. Bribes had already been paid for the gates to be opened, timed while everyone within would be at morning prayers, and the prince would be taken on the authority of my presence. By the end of the day, we would both be safely at Edinburgh Castle. It would require much travel for me, but for one day only, unlike the constantly moving progress James was on, and as the child I was carrying had not yet quickened, there was no risk of harm.

I told the courier I agreed and approved. After he'd left, Anna asked to see what he'd brought me. "He didn't leave it. Further adjustments are needed."

"What is it?"

"A gift for the king," I replied evasively. "I already told you that."

"What?" It was almost a demand.

"Stop questioning me," I said sharply. "It's to be a surprise. The more people who know about a surprise in advance, the less chance it succeeds in being one."

"Sometimes it's better for it not to," she said meaningfully.

The remaining hours of the day seemed endless, and it felt impossible for me to stay in my rooms until it was time to depart. I was restless, and longed to be among the courtiers who'd remained at the palace, either outside, or at dinner or supper, or even in the chapel. But I couldn't risk the possibility of news reaching James that I was up and about, and having him insist again that I visit Stirling. When I went there, it would be on my own terms in three days, and to take back my son. The thought of that being accomplished was sufficient to render my seclusion tolerable. As a diversion, I played endless games of cards with my women.

Those card games were undoubtably the cause of a strange dream I had that night, where I was playing one with James, Chancellor Maitland, and Anna. James and the chancellor were coolly polite to each other but veiling hostility, while Anna kept telling me it was a dangerous game I was playing. The rules of the game eluded me, and I grew increasingly anxious as I passed and accepted cards while trying to conceal I had no idea what I was doing. The more I tried to learn the rules, the more frustrated I became, and just as I was ready to sweep all the cards off the table, James held out his hands and stopped the game. Then the chancellor was gone, and James was bowing to Anna, saying, "Thank you." To me, he said, "That game is over!"

In the morning, I remembered it as soon as the curtain drew back and I saw Anna's face. "We won't be playing cards today," I said as I got out of bed. "And I think I'll feel better if

I'm out of these rooms. We'll go to chapel and breakfast as usual." A pervasive feeling of agitation was about me, which I knew would become unbearable unless I disbursed it through distractions of some sort. If James learned I'd improved, I could stall responding to anything he requested until my plans were accomplished.

I prayed in the chapel, chatted during breakfast, and reviewed with my stewards my accounts and various other household matters, but the tension would not diminish. All sorts of concerns hammered away at me: suppose the four groups failed to converge as planned? Suppose the bribes had failed and the gates weren't opened? What if we met with armed resistance at Stirling Castle and couldn't overcome it? I considered various responses to each potential problem, and all seemed woefully insufficient. My utter lack of knowledge of such situations was beginning to impress itself upon me, along with the full extent to which I was unprepared to contend with such an enterprise, and at the mercy of the abilities of others. For all that I was a queen, I had no experience of how to implement a solution to a problem extending beyond the court, even one that concerned the protection and well-being of my child. I doubted very much the English queen had ever found herself feeling the same, for if she had she would never have held her throne so long.

I was sure my unsettled mood was showing; my fingers fidgeted constantly, I was unable to sit still, and I spoke rapidly and continuously. I noticed my women eyeing me with concern, which only increased my discomfort.

With James's household gone, mine ate with me in a smaller banquet hall near my rooms. Late in the day we had begun supper when a bugle sounded, announcing an approach to the palace. A guard came and whispered to one of my women, who left her place at the table and came to me. "Your Grace," she said happily, her smiling face free of any guile, "the king is arriving!"

My back stiffened, and I felt the colour drain from my face. *James had found out.* I stared blankly ahead of me into the crowded room, where all continued to laugh and chatter as they ate, oblivious to the jarring shift of circumstances for me.

Just above me the woman's face hovered, her cheerful expression seeming to mock me. When she then said with enthusiasm, "We'll prepare the place beside you for the king!" it was all I could do to keep from slapping her. My world was on the verge of collapsing, and she was talking about table seating.

All at once a great weariness came over me. Slowly, with great effort, I pushed myself to my feet. Conversation in the room ceased, and everyone stood also. "Do whatever you want," I told the woman. "I don't care." As I left, I was sure all eyes were fixed on me.

Anna and the other women tried to follow me into my room. "Stay out!" I shouted at them, surprised I had the energy for it, for even closing the door on them seemed to require great strength. I dragged myself to the bed and dropped down onto it. It felt strange — I never did so fully dressed, with perfectly arranged hair, and wearing jewels. It was uncomfortable, but I barely noticed. *What will he say?* I thought dully. James was about to walk through the door. We had never before been at such a place in our marriage, and I had absolutely no idea what to expect of him, nor how to prepare a reply. My head was propped slightly up on the pillows, enough for me to look past the end of the bed, into the empty room, as I waited.

Presently I heard the door open, and then close. There were light, slow footsteps, and James came into view, still wearing his dark blue riding cloak and a tall, wide-brimmed hat, with a feather. He stopped at the foot of the bed and merely stood looking down at me, his expression calm. If he thought the sight of me sprawled across the bed wearing my finery was odd, he didn't show it.

For a long moment we stayed so, observing each other. Then he said, quietly, "You've been used by those who don't have your best interests at heart. Fortunately, there are others truly devoted to you, as well as me, and our child, and Scotland, who alerted me to this foolishness of taking Henry to Edinburgh. That plan has been stopped. There'll be no future recurrence."

I turned my head away from him. He went on, "You must be more careful in the future. Don't allow yourself to be the pawn of others. Maitland is a shrewd man."

At the mention of the chancellor, I turned back to him, meeting his gaze — a wordless acknowledgement of my involvement. When James spoke again, his words were angry: "Maitland's time has passed. His great power is no more. It has passed to me. Rather, I took it from him, having learned it from him, as was appropriate and right as I grew in understanding and ability. I am king, not he. Now, he resists it, as a father resists being replaced by his son. He forgets he was always my subject, his power borrowed from me, which he must now relinquish as I wield it myself. His efforts to reclaim it are foolish and useless."

James removed his hat, running his hand through his thick hair. Then he gave a short sigh. "He has managed to create some ripples through my council regarding Henry's care, which will take me more time to subdue. But even with your support, a change would not have happened. Now, once the others see neither you nor he are involved to champion their causes, it will dissolve completely. Maitland — once he saw I did not intend to remove him as chancellor — became very agreeable again, which pleases me. He has served both me and Scotland admirably for many, many years. I am not going to allow this poor decision of his to erase all that service."

Idly, he reached out and touched the nearest heavy bed curtain, gathered in the corner by the bedpost, and pushed it further back. "Anne, I in part blame myself for your having been drawn into this scheme. I've been insensitive to your sadness over the separation from Henry. I believed you of such mettle you would simply adjust to the absence — as I have. But I see now that your suffering has been to such an extent as to have clouded your intellect. I intend to change that. Shortly we depart for Stirling Castle, for a stay of a month."

I was to see my child again. In that instant, nothing else mattered. I would be with Henry again. Great relief came over me, and I closed my eyes.

"Anne," I heard James say, and opened them again. This time, without his hat, he looked less formidable, and his expression was softer. "You'll have an entire month to spend with Henry. But you must understand that we'll depart again at the end of that time. The arrangement can't be changed — especially not now, after this episode. It would, in fact, be even more difficult to alter than it was before. Your involvement has caused it to become a political matter. It is for all of us — me, you, Henry, and our unborn child — now of much greater significance."

He was telling me that what I had done had pushed me even further from what I had sought to achieve. Perhaps so, but I wondered what he would have said had I been successful.

Once again, I turned my face away from him. I heard his footsteps retreat across the room, and the door open and close.

Only then did I give way to tears, after which I got up and pulled off my gown and jewels and threw them on the floor. Hearing me, the women rushed in and helped me into a nightdress. I then got into bed, but didn't fall asleep until long after the daylight had faded into dark.

The next morning, when Anna came in, I said to her, "You were the one who told him, weren't you?" When she didn't reply, I went on, "You guessed I was planning with Maitland to take charge of the prince. And you thought me wrong, and went and told the king."

Still, she said nothing. But she didn't look away, her blue eyes meeting mine.

I continued, "You sought to protect me, but you didn't. Why do you of all people oppose me? You must think me a great fool. You behave as though you agree with James that I cannot have the care of my own child."

The other women started coming in with the morning's garments, but she waved them out. When the door had closed, I said, "I could have you banished from court. I could have you sent back to Denmark. Any other queen would. I won't. You are my friend, and I cannot do without you. But you must never go against me again, no matter how much you believe I am in error. I know you think that for me to go against my husband is wrong, that in Christian belief husband and wife stand together as one. But my son is a part of me also, and I cannot bear to be separated from him. You think my place as a wife takes precedence over that as a mother. I might have agreed with you before Henry was born, and before James took him from me. Now, I do not. You must trust that I am right. You form your opinion with thought and prayer. What you lack is the depth of my feelings. I am a wife and mother, and I feel this in ways you cannot."

I was sitting up in my bed. She knelt down beside me, took my hand and kissed it as she lay her head against my arm. And I knew that although she hadn't admitted it, she had indeed sent a message to James alerting him to my plans. But I could also tell that, whether she agreed with me or not, she would never do it again.

8

The exhaustion that had come over me with the collapse of my plans receded during the departure for Stirling, and vanished completely in the joy of my arrival there. James accompanied me in the coach, during which we were mostly silent but occasionally made polite but insignificant remarks to each other. As the castle's walls, rooftops and battlements appeared in the distance on Castle Hill, my excitement grew, and by the time we rode through the gatehouse into the lower courtyard it was nearly unmanageable. The entire castle staff had assembled there to greet us, in front of which stood the Earl of Mar and his mother. Between them, standing no taller than their knees, was Henry.

It was four months since I'd seen him, but it felt like a year. I could scarcely believe how tall he stood, and with such sober dignity for a child of sixteen months. Most startling, and clearly visible even from the coach window, was the extent to which he resembled me. His hair was as fair and thick as mine, and the shape of his face was the same.

A formal welcome had been prepared, but nothing could keep me longer from my child. As soon as the coach stopped, I pushed open the door and nearly jumped from it, and rushed forward to the tiny figure in the belted brocade green cloak that went all the way to his feet, with a little white ruff collar. He stood watching with great seriousness as I approached, his eyes the same shape and light blue colour as my own, and he neither flinched nor cried out as I gathered him up in my arms, kissing him repeatedly. Then I leaned back enough for us to see each other's faces, and he stared into my eyes, searchingly, but with recognition. One of his tiny hands reached up and rested gently on the side of my face.

I heard James speaking with the earl, saying something about dispensing with formalities. Vaguely, I was aware of the other coaches pulling up behind ours, and of Anna and the other women emerging, and coming forward to see Henry. But I would not share him with anyone. I'd known in an instant that the bond between us was still intact; he'd known me as his mother. It was a moment of such ecstatic relief that I was unwilling to release it. Carrying him, I moved past the assembled household staff and into the palace. Only inside did it occur to me that I had deprived James of his moment of reunion, for at best he'd been able to catch the briefest sight of the child in my arms. I took no pleasure in knowing he'd been so excluded.

My apartments had been readied, and in my bedroom, I finally set Henry down. He stood quietly as my women flocked in a circle around him, his interest taken by the rose satin of their swirling dresses. Two valets hurried in with the trunk containing the many toys I'd brought, all quietly gathered over the past weeks. I threw off my cloak and hat, knelt down and spoke to him gently as I opened the trunk and took out, one by one, the tops and balls and wooden toy soldiers and animals, intricately carved and colourfully painted. He watched, his blue eyes focused with interest, eagerly anticipating each gift, and taking it from me with his little hands. The one he liked best was the miniature sailing ship complete with sails, mounted on a base of wheels that could be pulled with a string.

Behind me, I heard James say, "He already prepares to command a fleet, one to be used to maintain peace. Unlike the Spanish, who build armadas for war. The great ship at his baptismal banquet was an omen of good fortune."

I stood up. It had been less than a year since that fantastical ship had been the centrepiece of the celebration welcoming Henry as heir to Scotland's throne, and likely England's as well. My happiness then had felt complete, and a blissful future had seemed to lie ahead of me. The last time I had been at Stirling, I had still been in that happy state, not knowing plans were already in place for my child to be taken from me, the first step of which had been my removal from the castle to Edinburgh. So shocking had that change been for me that it had overshadowed the deceptive way James had gone about it. Turning to him, I said pointedly, "The last time I occupied this bedroom, sir, my world had not yet shattered."

The silence that followed was pronounced, and seemed to extend beyond the walls of the room to include not only the entire castle, but all of Scotland as well. Everyone present — James, his gentlemen attendants, my gentlewomen, the Earl of Mar and his mother and their staff — knew that he had separated me from Henry without telling me. Many of them now, if not all, would also know that in the past few days, by similar deception, I had almost succeeded in reversing that situation. Staring directly at James, I continued, "We have returned here under quite different circumstances, haven't we?"

The silence continued, as though no one present even dared to breathe. James looked away from me, his eyes lowering to Henry, now sitting on the floor and playing with the ship. "Yet we are still king and queen," he said.

It was an indirect acknowledgement, before everyone, of what had passed between us — more than I thought he'd say. My bitterness receded, but only a little. "But not entirely as we were before," I answered.

He ignored the remark, instead coming forward and standing beside me, continuing to look down at Henry. "The prince has grown," he said. "He looks well. Stirling agrees with him as much as it did me when I was a child." Throughout the room were little murmurs of approval. Behind us, a masculine voice — likely the Earl of Mar's — said, "Thank you, Your Grace." Immediately the words were echoed by an older, female one, his mother's.

James praising them was intolerable. I said loudly, "As it agreed with Mary Stuart and Lord Darnley, before they married. But where did that good agreement lead?" A short, crisp laugh of derision escaped from my lips.

Somewhere in the room someone gasped audibly; then there was another moment of shocked silence. "A child should be with its mother," I said strongly.

"As he now is," James replied quietly. He reached down and touched Henry's head. "Learn the way of ships and the sea well, my son. There are times one must fight for peace."

Henry turned his face up to him, and I saw a recognition in his eyes similar to what I'd seen when he'd looked at me. He knew his father, and despite my bitterness, it pleased me. But when James abruptly broke the moment by standing up and turning away, I was not unhappy. The child's bond with me was stronger.

To the earl, James said, "Spain continues to harass England. Within a year another armada should be sent."

"Curse the Scottish papists!" someone in the room grumbled loudly. "Those who would have us ally with Spain."

The earl answered with dismissive disdain, "The new armada will suffer the same fate as the one seven years ago. The Spanish have small chance of victory, so long as Scotland continues to ally with England and offers them no haven." I wouldn't look at him as he spoke, although around the room there were remarks of agreement.

James, with smooth confidence, said, "Something my cousin Elizabeth understands all too well. As do the English people, in their growing respect and friendliness towards us. How better to cement such a friendship than for one ruler to unite both countries, ending forever the threat of foreign intervention on this island?" Abruptly, he turned to me, his eyes piercing. "Never forget the future we seek, for ourselves, or this child." His voice was strangely cold.

It was the closest thing to an additional rebuke he had uttered since the day of his unexpected return from Falkland Palace, and I knew it would be the last time he spoke about my failed plans. He had found a way to make a final point to me of the importance of his and my central positions among the struggles of nations. Undoubtably, it was so, but my having my child with me should in no way jeopardise them. "My being a queen does not stop me from being a mother. Nor should it stop you from being a father."

Before he could respond, I stepped away from him and told the valets to take the toy trunk to Henry's room, gesturing towards the door to the little room that had been used as his nursery.

But the earl raised his hand to stop them. "The prince's room is now in the old palace, Your Grace."

This time, I turned to face him. He wore black, as did his mother beside him, and he looked much older than James, his hair and beard both heavily greyed. He was also tall, like his mother, but heavier, and although his face was not so lined, it was equally as stern. There was an air of immovability about him.

"Why was he moved?" I demanded.

The countess said, "Without your presence, Your Grace, these rooms are unused. The prince had need of a larger suite. He now occupies the one beside my own."

"He should then have been moved to the king's apartments. Those which the king himself occupied as a child."

"No." James's words came fast. "He is not the king. I am. Those rooms are mine alone. The earl and the countess did well not to move him there." Then, almost in a whisper, he added, "There is only one king in Scotland."

He whirled around quickly, went to the earl, and took him by the arm. "My plans to hunt at Falkland were cut short. But I intend to make good use of the fine horses here, and the falcons." And without another word to me he strode from the room, followed by the earl and his attendants.

I wanted to run after him, to argue that our child was not well housed, and that his comments about him being a prince and not a king reeked of jealousy, which was ridiculous. But Henry was holding his ship and looking up at me, with the same seriousness he'd displayed since our arrival. "You need to smile, my child," I said, as I once again knelt down on the floor beside him. "We need to laugh and play." And I reached into the trunk and brought out more toys.

Over the next week, he did smile and laugh, more and more often. I put from my mind the knowledge that our time together wasn't permanent, and delighted in what we had. Every morning his attendants brought him to my apartments so that he was already with my women when I awoke. He accompanied me to the daily prayer services, where he sat solemnly beside me, and to breakfast with my household, and to dinner and supper in the banquet hall. At breakfast he sat on my knee and I fed him myself; at dinner and supper he sat on the other side of James, the courtiers doting on him. He was merriest when with me, becoming immediately lively every time he laid eyes on me. He spoke more, and although still only gibberish and babble, it was like sweet music to my ears.

Begrudgingly, I came to see that he was thriving in his home at Stirling. The earl and old countess wisely stayed at a distance, but I became acquainted with the staff, and very quickly saw they were devoted to him. Most of them were Murrays, relatives of the countess. After initially holding back, I began to respond to their demonstrations of loyalty and affection for Henry.

During the first week a quantity of clean napkins for me to cover my dress when holding Henry were delivered to my bedroom. "They're from the keeper of the linen," Anna told me. "She's one of the Murrays."

The gesture showed a courtesy beyond what my own women had thought of. "Send for her so I can thank her," I said.

The tall, unremarkable-looking woman who arrived wasn't young but not yet middle-aged. There were no airs or pretence of refinement about her, nor any religious stridency. As we spoke, I found a frankness in her that I liked. Over the following days we met several more times as she went about her tasks, and I spoke with her, but was careful the other staff wouldn't notice I had particularly singled her out — which I had. I needed to have someone there who would report to me how Henry fared after I departed, and who would alert me to any problems.

"The old woman's really not so bad," she confided after two weeks had passed, referring to the countess. "A lot of all that pious sternness is just for show, although she may not even know it herself, she's had to do it for so long. Religion is all mixed up with politics here in Scotland, and everyone has to make a show of it. But when she's not around you or the king or any nobles, she's more like an everyday woman. That's how she is around the prince. She's kind to him."

"And what of the earl?"

"He's always the earl," she said wryly. "His mother's old, and you can see at times she's not so interested in any of it anymore. But he still is, and wants to hold on to what he's got. He's got the king's friendship, and isn't about to let go of it. He'll do whatever the king wants. Taking care of the prince is just another job for him. But he hardly ever comes to see him in person, so his callousness won't affect him."

Faster than I could have believed, the visit was over. All the misery I'd held back during my time there came washing over me, and I could barely contain it in front of Henry as I said goodbye. My being able to at all was only because I now had my secret ally there to keep me directly informed. Hopefully the small bag of gold coins I was leaving with her would ensure it. Also, the report that the countess was more human than her imposing demeanour suggested had reduced my fears for my child's circumstances. But my resentment of the Earl of Mar, and James's support of him, continued unabated.

We were going to Falkland Palace. James said it was to finish his interrupted visit, but I knew it was also because it was far from Edinburgh and the chancellor's political plans. I'd overheard James, after receiving and opening a letter from Edinburgh, remark to the earl that certain lords now wanted the council to review Henry's residence and guardianship. The earl had replied, "Maitland's an old dog!" and James had answered, "Too old to bite hard enough," but when he'd seen me listening, he'd said nothing more. The exchange had given me hope, but not enough to hold off the overwhelming loss that gripped me in the coach as Stirling Castle receded behind us.

Falkland Palace had been a hunting lodge, before being expanded by James's grandfather in a French chateau style. It was made of grey stone and was low and spreading, with many graceful curves. Inside, the rooms were not as large and grand as the other royal residences, and although beautifully decorated, not as formal. It was still ideal for hunting, on the edge of a huge forest of oaks, full of deer and wild boar, and there was a tennis court, and lovely gardens, orchards and meadows for walking. Mary Stuart had favoured it, not only as a reminder of her youthful days in France, but because of the sports she so loved, especially tennis. She'd excelled at it, but unfortunately, her agility and strategy hadn't carried over into more important parts of her life.

The summer foliage was in bloom, enhancing the charm of the landscape as we approached the palace. But I turned away from the coach window as we rode through the cheering residents on the streets of the attached village, and immediately retreated to my bedroom after we passed through the gatehouse. The beauty of the palace and its setting did not ease the emptiness within me. I sent a message to James that I wouldn't be at supper, and went to bed.

Hours later I was jolted awake by severe cramps through my lower body. As I sat up in the darkness, struggling to throw off the disorientation of sleep, I was seized by more, and I felt a discharge. Without looking, I knew it would be blood. I screamed for my women, but even before Anna yanked back the bed curtains and the flickering candlelight showed the dark red stain on my nightdress, I knew it was too late.

Anna was shouting for the physicians, and those of my women who'd borne children were pushed forward to the end of the bed, where they stood as though rigid with fear, their eyes wide. "Lie flat," one of them whispered, and I did, feeling the discharge increasing, with more substance.

When the first physician arrived, rushing to the bed in his long nightgown, I said to him, "Too late."

The look on his face showed I wasn't mistaken. "I'm afraid so, Your Grace," he said quietly. Behind him, some of the women began to sob.

"Go away, all of you," I said in a low voice. The pain was decreasing, replaced by exhaustion like that which had come over me at Linlithgow with the collapse of my plans. Only this time it was much worse.

"We must attend to you," the doctor said gently, and asked me to describe what I was feeling.

I feel like I've given birth but have nothing to show for it. "Empty," was all I could manage to reply. I stared at the top of the bed and wanted nothing more than to be left alone in the darkened room.

For two weeks I would not speak to anyone, not James or Anna or the physicians or any of the clergymen who offered me 'solace'. I barely rose from the bed, spending entire days and nights there, sometimes sleeping but often not, my mind strangely dull. At first, I refused food also, until one of the older cooks brought a stew especially for my 'troubles', as she said to Anna, who brought her to where I sat slumped in a chair beside the bed. The aroma of the meats and seasonings was strong, at first nauseating me and causing me to turn my head away. But the woman persisted, saying, "Come, Your Grace, you must eat and get strong. Do you think you're the first woman to lose a child before its time? You're a strong woman, and you'll have more, if you'll keep your strength up and not curl up in a corner to die like an old cat." She shoved the bowl towards my face, nearly touching my nose.

"That's enough," Anna told her warningly.

"What happens to her son if she lets herself die?" the woman asked with gruff and hearty sincerity. "There's no replacement for a child's mother!" She bent forward, peering directly into my face, and commanded, "Eat!"

Anna reached out to pull her away, but the woman's words had broken through my melancholy haze. I took the bowl and spoon and began to eat as though ravenous. She waited until I'd finished, Anna silent by her side. When I thrust the empty bowl back at her, she said, "Now, that's what I would expect from a queen. I'll bring you something else, later. And herbs all the women take for times like this. Nothing your grand doctors will give you, only things we find in the woods. But you'll be up and about in no time at all."

And so I ate and felt stronger, and although I still wouldn't speak, I began to think more. I'd overheard the physicians telling James that the long coach trip from Stirling might have been the cause, although it shouldn't have because there'd been no quickening yet. It was surprising also, because I'd carried Henry without incident or trouble. Had I, they asked, been unhappy lately, or coping with some difficulty? James hadn't replied, but he had to have known the answer was yes, as much as I knew it. And I wondered if he felt himself to blame.

The first few words I spoke, more than a week later, were to Anna: "Does James blame himself for the unhappiness that caused the miscarriage?"

I'd expected she would be pleased at my having found my voice again. But instead she asked sternly, "Do you blame yourself? Perhaps you should. It was poorly considered to allow yourself such a temper over your husband's decision, and while blessed by God with the possibility of another child. Perhaps it was God's will for the child not to be born; his ways are mysterious and we do not understand them. Perhaps it would have been lost even had you been happy, and taken the utmost care. But it is not fair of you to blame the king. His decision may not have been the best, but you made the matter worse. You put the insult to yourself and your anger ahead of the best interests of the child you were carrying. You cannot blame the king any more than yourself."

Her audacity was shocking, and I turned away and silently vowed I would never speak to her again, or anyone else. But I couldn't shake the thought that what she had said was true, and if she had thought of it, so had everybody else, including James. In addition to my being viewed with sympathy by the court, they would also see me as a great fool who had sacrificed the possibility of a second child in pursuit of control over the first.

The next morning, I got up as usual and resumed my daily routine. When James saw me, he responded as though I'd been absent for no more than a day. Melancholy still clung to me, and everyone seemed to understand that I didn't want to join in with conversation or activities. I spoke little and neither smiled nor laughed. But being among others was bearable again, and my misfortunes and disappointments no longer felt so overwhelming.

As the weeks of the summer passed, I began to walk in the gardens, and later the meadows and orchards. My physicians were pleased with my progress and soon I was allowed to ride again. But I held back from joining James on the hunts in the forest, or from watching him play tennis. We were polite when we encountered each other at chapel or at dinner and supper. Reports he received from Stirling were immediately passed on to me. Henry had begun talking, his words careful and slow. Although not hearing them still caused me great sadness, my fears over his well-being had decreased since our visit. His circumstances were agreeable, his attendants devoted and kind, and I now had a secret ally in the linen keeper. Not least of all, I no longer thought the countess the horror I had at first.

But the superior and condescending way I'd been treated by James still made me angry; I'd struggled with him, and he'd won. There were times over the summer when I drifted into thinking of him with familiar love and fondness, but I ruthlessly stopped them. There'd been a change between us, and I was uncertain how to continue with him.

One afternoon in the first week of October, he came to where I was sitting in the garden and sent all our attendants away, and I knew a turning point had arrived. Anxiety seized me, but faded beneath a more powerful relief that at least from today there would be clarity between us.

"Maitland is dead," he began. "He died in his sleep at Thirlestane Castle. God was satisfied with him, to let him die at home in his own bed. He'd gone there from Edinburgh a week ago, when the first signs of his illness took him."

It was not as startling as it usually was when I heard of the unexpected death of another. Before leaving Linlithgow, James had told me the chancellor had been trying to recapture his power, which was finished. If his place in life had truly been lost, and he was too old to establish another, it wasn't surprising death had taken him.

The clear sunlight and beauty of the garden around us spoke of life, the touches of early autumn promising a bountiful harvest. A canopy had been arranged over the chairs that had been set out, and James now sat down beside me. He said, "I intend to do without a chancellor. Scotland is not so large that I need one, now that I am competent. Whoever I chose would rival me, as Maitland did. I've no need for anyone to stand beside me as I rule — except you." Overhead, a slight breeze rippled the canopy. "You resent the influence of the Earl of Mar. But you need not. I have affection for him and his family from my childhood, and I trust them. I need them now to protect the prince. But their influence doesn't extend beyond that. I intended to establish a different household for the child we expected, with a different guardian — a Catholic one."

We'd been looking at each other, and my eyes widened with surprise.

"Yes," he said. "All our children must have separate households. If disaster struck, we wouldn't all be eliminated."

All our children, I thought. *He still intends for us to have more. He had no doubt we would reconcile.* I sat perfectly still, making no gesture of refusal or agreement.

He continued, "It is imperative that our line go on. You and I are to found a dynasty to rule over all of Britain and maintain peace within it, and influence Europe for the same good. Our children must be kept safe, and we must have many of them. The loss of the —" he hesitated — "expected one was a heavy disappointment."

I looked away, down to his hands. For the first time I understood the loss had been devastating for him also. I'd been so sunken in my own unhappiness that I'd never considered he could be deeply affected.

He briskly wiped his hands together, as though brushing dust off them, and said tensely, "Henry's placement with a Calvinist was important, not only for him, but for all of us, and the next child's placement with a Catholic will be equally so. I must always balance these struggling Scottish factions, who now, in religion, have found something else to use against each other." Frustration sounded in his voice, and I looked back at his face. "Catholics and Calvinists. Sometimes I wonder about the truth of any of it. I even wonder if we continue at all, after life. But I do know we continue through our children. For you and I to accomplish that, for our lives to be of lasting meaning, we need each other."

His voice became quieter, gentler, but his words were quicker, as though he were reluctant to speak them but feared that if he didn't, he might not ever be able to. "I need you beside me, to complement me where you excel and I am lacking. I'm awkward and clumsy and without charm. I have none of what is called 'style'. Here in Scotland this isn't so noticeable a failing, but what of in England? In such a land of sophistication, beauty and culture to rival any in Europe? My anxiety is great when I consider this, for a sovereign must in every way appear the part. The only relief I have to my fear is the knowledge that you would be at my side."

He'd never spoken to me so before, telling me I was important not only as the mother of his children, but in my own right. What he said was true; I did have excellent taste, and a sense of beauty and style. My abilities might not be so needed in Scotland, but he was correct that they would be essential in England. There would be a cultural landscape to influence and develop, as well as a political one. And he needed me to do it.

I looked out over the garden, resplendent in the dazzling sunlight, but instead of seeing it I saw the years ahead, full of creative and beautiful enterprises. As Queen of England I would have undreamed-of opportunities to influence art, architecture, dance, drama and literature. I would be able to help shape a culture, as James would shape a modern world.

"We must achieve the English throne," James said quietly. "No matter how strong our prospects, nothing is in hand until it is ours. You and I must work together, and not be divided by differences. What better gift could we give to Henry, and the children to come?"

The future visions faded. Once again it was the garden before me, still lovely in early autumn colours, but still only a garden in Scotland. It was time for me to make a decision. Henry was safe at Stirling, with attendants who were kind and devoted. I would never like not having him with me, but with effort, I might learn to tolerate it.

I looked back at James and found him staring at me, waiting for my response. He hadn't apologised for the depth to which his behaviour had hurt me, but he'd told me he valued my presence, in ways that were not subordinate. If not everything, it was something.

After a moment, I said, "The day is so fine we should make the most of it. More of the summer's flowers have lingered further down. Shall we go and see them, together? But we need to be careful, for the path is uncertain in places."

"Yes," he agreed. "Let us walk a while." We both stood up. He offered his arm, and I rested my hand on his.

9

"Mr Heriot is here," Anna said, "with the gifts for your children."

December 1602 had started with rain but no snow, which I hoped would hold off at least until January. At the end of the month all three children were to visit us at Holyrood Palace for the New Year celebration, and bad weather could prevent their coming, especially Charles, who at two was frailer than his older siblings, and whose household at Dunfermline was the most distant. Six-year-old Elizabeth was closest at Linlithgow, and she also had a stubborn streak that would leave her undeterred from setting out in the worst of snowstorms to visit Edinburgh, which even at so young an age she loved. And Henry, at eight, less stubborn than his sister but bolder and more adventurous, would find a storm exciting and a trip through bad weather from Stirling Castle a challenge, even though the sophisticated metropolis held no particular appeal for him as a destination. But all of their guardians were rigorously careful of their health and safety, and wouldn't hesitate to cancel the trip at the first signs of approaching bad weather. For all my hopes and prayers, the visit was something I couldn't be sure of until it happened, for the winters of southern Scotland, although usually mild and without much snow, were changeable, and travel plans could be altered at the last moment.

"Show Mr Heriot in," I told Anna, gesturing to the little room where we sometimes ate. "The table is large enough for him to show the trinkets."

She went to get him, and I went to the inner room. It was comfortable and snug, its colourful tapestries showing summer scenes, and a cosy fire helping dispel the dreariness of the morning. Although it was after nine o'clock, dawn came late in December, and the sun, barely present behind grey clouds, was still newly risen.

I asked one of my gentlewomen to light the candelabra on the table, and the room became even more cheerful. Long ago I'd overcome my aversion to its having been the site of the murder of Mary Stuart's secretary Rizzio. No matter what association James's parents had with Holyrood Palace, the apartments they had occupied were now ours. Mary Stuart and Lord Darnley and their unfortunate lives were in the past, and memories of them were best banished.

Mr Heriot came in, looking barely older than when I'd first met him, his fair hair still untouched by grey, his smooth face without lines of age or worry. "Your Grace," he said, bowing. "I've brought the Hogmanay gifts."

With effort I prevented myself from wincing visibly. *Hogmanay* was as ugly a name for a New Year celebration as I could imagine, equal to the ugliness of the decision of the Calvinist clergy to ban Christmas celebrations. The loss of those sweet and ancient rituals from my Lutheran childhood had been jarring in my first year in Scotland, and I'd never adjusted to their replacement with the non-religious, briefer and less colourful Hogmanay. My dislike had only worsened after bearing children, when my appreciation of Mary's maternal importance had begun; of all the holy days, Christmas seemed most connected to her. Fortunately, Elizabeth and Charles had Catholic guardians, who privately continued to celebrate the holiday. But Henry, at Stirling, was deprived by the staunch Calvinism of the Earl of Mar. The clergy and the people of Scotland watched us closely, and James and I could do nothing to upset the balance between the religious factions. I had no choice but to conform to the religion of the state, and observe its practices, and I couldn't even create a belated small, private Christmas for Henry when he arrived. The best I could do was a generous gift for all three on Hogmanay, and I consoled myself that in England the holiday was still enthusiastically celebrated. Sooner or later, the English throne would come to us, and we would live there.

I sat down at the table, and Mr Heriot began unwrapping the gifts: ten gold and silver toy soldiers for Henry; a gold-backed hairbrush for Elizabeth, engraved with the initial E; and a small silver horse on four gold wheels for Charles. All were delightful and exquisitely made. I gave the horse a little push, and it rolled nearly halfway across the table, stopped by the upright soldiers, who stood their ground. I couldn't help but laugh. "Such wonderful gifts," I said. "As usual, I am more than pleased, Mr Heriot."

"Thank you, Your Grace. I will leave them with you today. The prince and princess and the duke are sure to appreciate their mother's generosity."

"Forward the bill to my steward, as usual."

"Certainly." He began folding the silk wrappings around each. "I have also brought something else I thought might be of interest to you."

"You always do, Mr Heriot."

"I consider it an obligation to be constantly alert for anything that might appeal to my queen, either for yourself or as a fine gift for another."

With any other merchant I'd have disliked the self-interest, but with him I didn't. He knew I liked jewellery, an interest that had blossomed over the years. A new, beautifully wrought ring, brooch, bracelet or necklace brought me a thrill and longing that could be satisfied only by making it mine. Enhancing my wardrobe had also become a great interest, and I was now the best client of many of the dressmakers and milliners of Edinburgh. I never exceeded my budget; it wouldn't do for stories to circulate of the queen being in debt. But I was rich, and my budget was very large indeed, so mostly I spent what I wanted and was happy doing so. There were occasional remarks of dislike at court and from the clergy, but I ignored them. Suggestions of selfishness were few and rare, especially since it was well known that I was generous in my gifts to others.

"So what have you to show me today?" I asked.

Mr Heriot slid aside the three gifts on the table, and reached into his tunic to produce another, much smaller package. My eyes remained fixed on his slender hands as he delicately unwrapped the red silk and produced a heavy gold ring, made for a man. I took it from him and held it closer to see its details, admiring its rubies shaped into hearts. It was a beautiful ring, and would make a fine gift for James. Years ago, he'd given me a similarly designed brooch, and it would be suitable for husband and wife to wear such pieces. But that gift had been tied to my separation from Henry.

I must have frowned, because Mr Heriot asked, "You do not care for it?"

I held it in my open palm, as though weighing it. For all that James and I had reconciled, and experienced happy years since, the sense of unity from the first years of our marriage had only partly been regained. Lingering small resentments served as reminders that it had never been the same. Back then, I would have bought the ring.

"I've spent too much already," I said, returning it to him. "I can't afford a gift for the king."

Mr Heriot took it, and our eyes met. I saw something in his that said he understood that I had other, deeper reasons for turning it down, reasons I would never discuss with him. As he was folding it back into the silk, I suddenly said, "Show it to me again at some later time. But it's not for now."

He changed the subject. "You haven't requested a gift for Queen Elizabeth this year. Are you giving money? I understand most of her court does."

"We've heard she still enjoys a gift. The gold cup you created last year pleased her greatly. This year we've chosen something more elaborate, but not a jewel or cup, which is why you haven't heard from me. We're giving her a cloak."

"A cloak," he repeated softly, his brown eyes widening with curiosity. He knew that if it was for Queen Elizabeth, it was bound to be more than a usual garment, and the artisan in him was pleasantly intrigued.

With some pride, I explained, "I designed it myself. It's intricately embroidered with flowers and birds of many colours, shot with thread of gold, and trimmed with carnation velvet. The background is mostly a rich, deep red. It's something so fantastic it could never be worn in Scotland. But we have it on good authority that Elizabeth has increasingly favoured such garments, and surprisingly, given her age, wears them well." I paused. "I wish I could show it to you, but it's already been sent to our ambassador in London for presentation on New Year's Day. You certainly would appreciate the effort that has gone into it."

"It sounds magnificent, Your Grace. And expensive."

"It was very much so, and it shows. We wanted the value to be clear, as a sign of how much we esteem our cousin. But just as much, we wanted the English court to understand that Scotland isn't barbaric. We have taste and style here, although our opportunities for display aren't so great as in England."

Mr Heriot smiled knowingly. "A wise decision. I would guess the idea originated with you, rather than the king."

It flattered me that he thought so. "It did. But the king liked it, and found the finished garment delightful." James had been greatly appreciative, and direct in telling me so. For years we'd regarded anything that moved us closer to the English throne to be of central importance, and had together worked smoothly and harmoniously to achieve it. Our efforts hadn't waned, despite Queen Elizabeth's surprising longevity; she'd lived into her late sixties with robust good health and vitality. Her eventual death was something she'd never been willing to discuss, but her counsellors and the leading English peers had quietly made it known to us that James would succeed her, and if she wouldn't overtly endorse the plan, neither had she opposed it. James and I had been encouraged to foster a closeness with her without mentioning it, and for the past few years we'd regularly exchanged letters. Meanwhile, there were signs throughout England that the change would be welcome. Its prosperity had begun to tatter around the edges, the conflict with Spain that had peaked with the Armada having dragged on without resolution, and the economy having suffered from several years of failed harvests. Balancing the ever-present religious conflicts there was more difficult than in Scotland. Part of the appeal of James as successor was the stability he'd achieved between the Calvinists and the Catholics, and he'd quietly offered assurances to both sides in England that no one would be persecuted because of religion; so long as Catholics were quiet, they wouldn't be troubled. We would conform to the Anglican state religion and follow its practices, not only with the daily services but in the celebration of holidays. Dispensing with the Scottish Hogmanay and having Christmas again was something I eagerly looked forward to.

I thanked Mr Heriot for his efforts, and he left. Then I called Anna and gave her the three gifts to put away until the end of the month. "Don't you want to know what they are?" I asked.

"I can wait," she answered. Her expression looked set, with a practised blankness. In recent years, it was a look she'd displayed more and more, as her general appearance had become plainer, her dress and bonnet simpler, often black, although still of good velvet and taffeta. I'd always allowed her not to wear my livery if she chose not to, and more and more she hadn't. Jewellery and ribbons had vanished from her attire. She'd also become more reserved, involving herself less in games and sports with me and the other gentlewomen. Instead, she read and was often at prayer. Although she never said so, I was sure she'd become a Catholic, finding beauty and colour in an elaborate inner world while her outer one became more austere. Increasingly, I feared she would leave and go to France to become a nun.

I told her Mr Heriot had suggested a gift for James. "He showed me a beautiful ring, of gold and rubies. But I declined it. The Hogmanay presents are only for the children. There are other times that he and I give each other gifts."

She looked away from me, and then back, as though she wanted to speak but wasn't sure she should.

"What?" I asked. "If you have something you want to tell me, go ahead."

"You and the king only give each other gifts formally, as though it's an obligation. You used to do so with true feeling."

My reply came sharp and quick: "We were young then. It's different between us now."

"You buy much for yourself. But jewels and clothing can't make up for love."

I was shocked. "How dare you say that to me! You overstep! The king and I are in perfect harmony. And what a thing for you, who knows nothing of love, to say. You, who refuse to even consider marriage!"

She ignored my agitation. "The birth of Prince Henry divided you and the king," she said plainly. "You continue to harbour anger over his being taken from you."

I stood up, pushing the chair back, the sound of its legs scraping on the floor loud in the room. "Yes!" I exclaimed, hitting my open palms on the table, and leaning towards where she stood, perfectly still and clutching the children's gifts. "It was a terrible loss for me! But I have put it in the past. It's ridiculous for you to suggest I'm still angry, and even more so to say I seek garments and jewels as a substitute. I've lost nothing, and don't appreciate your saying so. Indeed, I forbid you to ever speak such foolishness again, to anyone."

She could have argued with me — she had, many times before, and she knew I never held it against her. But this time she didn't. She simply curtsied and left the room.

She's unhappy, I thought after the door closed behind her. *It's why she's turned more into herself, and into religion, over the years.* She'd be different if she'd married and had children. For all that James and I at times disagreed, I still believed I'd made the right decision marrying him. Old Queen Elizabeth alone on her throne waiting for her eventual demise could at times produce a response of outright horror within me. Even more than marriage, it was children which gave one satisfaction in life, even when at times loss and sorrow entered one's life through them.

I went back into my bedroom and sent the women there into the outer room with the others. As soon as I was alone, I opened a little trunk I always kept on a table beside the bed whenever we changed residences. From it I withdrew a linen purse, and took out two small golden spoons and a tiny velvet hood. The spoons had been Hogmanay gifts for my daughter Margaret, born two years after Elizabeth, and who'd lived barely long enough for two new year celebrations to pass. The hood had been worn by Robert, born less than a year ago and surviving only four months, not even long enough to receive a Hogmanay gift.

I wiped away the inevitable tears and held the three mementoes, gently and lovingly. From birth neither child had been strong, and their early departures from life had been expected. Still, the losses had been difficult for both James and myself, and I'd been left with complicated feelings of unfairness and deprivation as well as sadness. Only the existence of the other children had been a consolation, along with the knowledge and hope there could still be more.

After several moments I placed the spoons and hood back in the pouch, and into the trunk. But this time as I closed the lid I did so with less sorrow than the last time I'd looked at them. My course had not arrived in October or November. If December passed without it, I could with confidence tell James I was with child again, a Hogmanay gift for both of us.

Hogmanay arrived with the midnight ringing of all the church bells in Edinburgh, and fireworks vivid against the black sky. From a large upper window, we watched the immense torch-bearing crowd swarm through the palace's distant outer gate to offer us good wishes for the new year. The approaching torchlight expanded through the thick darkness, faces and bodies, heavily garmented against the cold, becoming distinct as they drew near. The wildness was a little frightening, but neither Henry nor Elizabeth displayed any sign of intimidation, standing with perfect poise and dignity between James and me at the window. Behind them, Charles slept in his nurse's arms, indifferent to the bells and the fireworks, and the cheers and greeting cries of the crowd.

"They've reached the guards," Henry said, without turning from the window. His tone was hushed, but still managed to convey that he'd like nothing better than to be outside with them, carrying a torch.

The guards stood several yards from the entrance, but close enough for the crowd to see us clearly at the window. James and I wore our crowns and the two older children their coronets, all made of gold heavily encrusted with jewels. Behind and beside us, servants held candelabras so our appearance would be clear, a living portrait for the crowd of their royal family. Further off in the room the court was gathered, mostly Calvinists, the Catholics having chosen to stay home to quietly celebrate the traditional Christmas holidays. *How many of the court,* I wondered, *as well as those outside in the crowd, secretly miss those ancient celebrations, like I do? How many would have preferred gently flickering Christmas candles and sweet holy music to the torches and boisterous cries and cheers?*

"They've seen us," Elizabeth said excitedly. "They're pointing and waving. Should we wave back?" She looked up at me, her beautiful face so similar to mine, but still not so much as Henry's was. Her hair was darker, too. Of the three children, only Charles resembled James, and even at two years old it was clear he would have the same heavily lidded eyes.

"Look back to the window, child," James answered, and she did at once. He went on, "We will all wave presently, when the crowd is closer to the guards and can see us."

"The men wanting to be first-footer are pushing to the front," Henry announced. "I can see them!"

"Where?" asked Elizabeth. "How can you tell who they are?"

"Look for tall men," he explained quickly, "without hat or hood to show their dark hair. The crowd will choose and push one forward."

Outside the calls recognising us had become strong and loud. "Wave," James said, and we all did, causing the cries and cheers to increase to a deafening roar of approval. I heard him snap his fingers, the signal for the courtiers, who rushed forward to the other windows. We watched as those in the crowd closest to the front entrance tussled with each other, and other men further back still struggled forward. To be chosen first-footer was considered as lucky for him as for us, and competition for the honour was fierce and bold.

Finally, a man emerged in front of the guards, a tall one with the expected dark hair. "First-footer," James said loudly, as though the man could hear him. "May you bring us luck by your entrance into our home." All around the courtiers voiced their own good wishes for us. Outside, the Captain of the Guards hurried over to the man, spoke with him, then stepped back as he strode forward and out of sight below us, his actual entrance hailed by cheers and cries of *First-footer!* and *First footer into the King's house!* from the crowd.

"Wave again," James ordered, and we did, and the cries and cheers sounded louder. Then I took each child by the hand, and with the nurse holding the baby, retreated from the window, the courtiers falling back with us. For a moment James stood there alone, then waved again. There was another roar from the crowd, then he turned and joined us, all the courtiers circling round.

"So, we greet another year," he said to me serenely, his expression satisfied. "May the first-footer bring us the luck to make it a good one."

The steward who attended to our jewels stepped up with four servants, who deftly removed our crowns and coronets, and hurried out with them. Henry especially appeared gratefully relieved of a burden, and shook his head and tossed back a lock of hair that had fallen down on his forehead. Then he said with authority, as though answering an unasked question, "First-footer must always be a dark-haired man, because the Vikings who used to trouble Scotland were fair." There was a surprised silence, during which everyone stared at him; outside, the sound of the crowd was diminishing. He calmly added, "I am as fair-haired as any Viking. Had I been one, I'd have been the most ferocious of all. But I'd have left Scotland in peace."

Delighted laughter rang out among the courtiers, and one called out, "Scotland would have been fortunate for that, Your Grace!"

Clearly emboldened by the approving response to her brother's words, Elizabeth said, "I am nearly as fair as Henry, and I'd have been a Viking too. Even though I don't know what a Viking is."

Gales of laughter sounded around us. When it was sufficiently quiet, I said, "Perhaps you would have been. Your cousin Queen Elizabeth proved a warrior to equal the best of the Vikings, using her wits as weapons to defeat her Spanish foes."

"Ugh, the Spanish," said Henry, wrinkling his handsome little nose. "Don't even say the name!"

This time, the laughter was even stronger. James's eyes closed halfway, showing he was thinking. As the laughter receded, he said evenly, "I am fair-haired also, yet I thank God I have never been a man of war. I have the same Tudor wits as my cousin Elizabeth, but mine are used in the preservation of peace. I am no heathen Viking."

Henry looked up at him and frowned. "My lord father, your hair isn't fair. It's grey."

A few courtiers laughed again, but not all; they watched us closely for cues as to how to respond. James stared at Henry, then fondly placed his hand on his head. "When I was younger mine was fair, but not so fair as yours, which is more like your mother's."

"His Grace's greying hair is a sign of his wisdom," someone said, followed by murmurs of approval.

"And yet I was born old," James said, wistfully. His hand, heavily ringed, still rested on Henry's head, and although the child did not move, his face showed he found it as heavy as the coronet he'd just been relieved of. He turned his face upward towards James, causing the hand to slide off.

"My lord father, if we despise heathens, why do we celebrate Hogmanay?" he asked. "My tutors have said it is from a pagan tradition."

The courtiers were tensely silent, watching for James's response. The answer to the simple question was a complex one, involving the break from Catholicism, and requiring political delicacy so as not to have the Calvinist clergy appear hypocritical.

Before James could reply, a female voice further back in the room, behind the circle of courtiers, asked, "Is the pagan Hogmanay better to celebrate than the Catholic Christmas, which the Scottish clerics despise as popery? Are Calvinists and Catholics not both Christians?"

My entire body tensed, not only because of the truth of the words, but because I recognised the voice as Anna's. Urgently, I cast about for something to say to redirect everyone's attention, but I couldn't think of anything. Then, to my great relief, Charles shifted in his nurse's arms, and snored loudly. All eyes turned to him, and in the next instant, laughter followed.

"The children should all be in bed," I said when it stopped, reaching down and taking Henry and Elizabeth by the hand.

At that moment, the Earl of Mar pushed through the courtiers, went to James and whispered in his ear. Again, fear touched me, for I'd long believed him oppositional to me, and influential in Henry's removal from my care. But as a smile appeared on James's face, my concern vanished.

James said, "It appears this year's first-footer is a visitor from England." He said nothing else, and there was a tiny pause, but then everyone applauded. They had understood that it suggested the new year would bring us the English throne.

Anna's remarks were forgotten, and she followed me as I hurried away, holding the children's hands. But in the corridor, Elizabeth asked what popery was.

"Followers of the Pope," Henry answered before I could. "The Catholics." His tone matched the one in which he had earlier mentioned the Spanish, as though he despised them.

"Those are matters you don't understand yet," I told them, and looked back over my shoulder to stare harshly into Anna's face. If Elizabeth had heard the remarks, so had everyone else, and we were fortunate for the interruption that had diverted attention away from them.

10

The children had all been given their own rooms, where their attendants now waited for them. I sent the princes to theirs, saying I'd be in to say goodnight, and went first with Elizabeth into hers. Her gentlewomen, many of whom had been with us, watching the first-footer ritual, had hurried back and were waiting with her nightdress ready, and the covers turned down on her bed. I waved them away, telling them to wait in the corridor with my own women. "I will attend the princess myself, tonight," I said. The children would leave again in the morning, and I wanted to spend as much time with them as I could.

As they hurried out, Elizabeth looked at me in surprise. "But my lady mother, will you know what to do?"

I laughed and set about helping her out of her gown, of dark red velvet with white satin sleeves, trimmed with gold. It was a near match to the one I was wearing, and I'd had it made especially for her, having received meticulous measurements from her guardians. She'd been thrilled with it, and even more so upon seeing the similarity to my own, when we'd both appeared in the banquet hall. Throughout dinner and the festivities that had filled the time before midnight, I had looked at her and seen myself at her age. I was full of pride at her progress. She danced exquisitely, and both recited and sang in a sweet, well modulated voice, and her manners were perfect.

"I was very proud of you tonight," I told her, as I dropped the dress on a chair, where her women could attend to it later. In her little petticoat she looked younger and less regal, like any Scottish six-year-old instead of a princess. She also seemed more fragile, and I knelt beside her and hugged her. She wrapped her arms around my neck and kissed me.

"Mother, could I not live here with you?" she asked.

I leaned back and held her at arm's length, staring into her face. "Now, why would you want to leave all your friends at Linlithgow? I thought you were very happy there?" But I was extremely pleased she'd made the request, for it said my child loved me and wanted to be near me.

Her face showed displeasure. "It becomes so dreadfully boring there," she pouted. "Here in Edinburgh there is so much more to do. But this visit is so short I have no time to go to the shops."

The mercenary reason, instead of the expected affirmation of love, was so innocently direct that I could not help but be charmed by it. I hugged her again and said, "You'll have many chances to shop in those places when you are older. Now come, we dally, and I must get you into your nightdress."

When the petticoat was off and the nightdress on, I pulled a small robe around her shoulders and had her sit before the dressing table. "Do you like the hairbrush?" I asked as I took it up. It was her Hogmanay gift, presented earlier.

"Very much," she answered, but as I ran it through her hair, her shoulders hunched together and she let out a little cry, causing me to stop at once. "That's not how my women do it," she said, with the slightest touch of reproach in her voice.

A feeling of failure, disproportionate to the moment, presented itself, because I didn't know how to brush my own daughter's hair. Resentment towards James leapt up in me, for if she'd been living with me, I certainly would know how. "I'm sorry," I said softly, setting the brush down on the table.

She swivelled round to look up at me, her expression deeply serious, concerned that she'd troubled me. "You're the queen!

Too important to be brushing anyone's hair." She stood up. "I'm sorry I asked to leave Linlithgow."

I sat down on the chair and drew her close, looking directly into her eyes. "Is it truly because you prefer the excitement of Edinburgh?"

Her eyes lowered. "No."

"Why, then?"

"Because Margaret died there."

The mention of her sister was startling, not only for the unexpected reminder of the two-year-old who hadn't survived, but because reports had been that Elizabeth had expressed little interest in her sister while they'd both lived there together. I'd assumed she'd been too young to have formed a bond with her. I touched her chin and gently lifted her face up towards mine again. "I'm so sorry to hear that. I didn't know you felt that way. Margaret's death was so sad for all of us. But you must know she hadn't been well for some time, and I'm afraid if she'd lived longer, she might never have been strong enough to enjoy her life." Suddenly and inexplicably, something prompted me to say, "We must try to be grateful for the time God gives us with each other."

I thought she might then mention Robert, the infant who'd more recently followed his sister, but she didn't. I was grateful, for I wasn't sure I knew how to respond. "I'm sorry you're not happy at Linlithgow," I said, "but I think it best if you return there." Remembering the first-footer had been English, I added encouragingly, "Although it may not be for much longer. I can't tell you why right now, but we all may be moving before long. Meanwhile, try to be happy there. You have everything you want, don't you? It's such a lovely castle; I think the loch must be beautiful in winter. And is the centre fountain covered over in ice?"

She replied that it was. Then she climbed onto my lap and rested her head against my shoulder. I waited for her to speak, perhaps to repeat her request to stay at Holyrood Palace with us, as I imagined I would have had I been her. But she didn't, and after several moments I found the silence awkward. "Your bedroom at Linlithgow must be very pretty," I said.

"This one is nicer." She said it plainly, without a hint that she was repeating her request to stay. Surely a child of six couldn't be so subtle. She was starting to feel heavy now, on my lap, and pressed against my shoulder.

I said, "This room is very nice, isn't it? I thought you would like it. I think it might have been used by the four Maries, the tapestries are so dainty and pretty. And this furniture is so light and delicate, more so than in any other room here."

"Who were the Maries?" she asked. "And why were there four of them?"

I hesitated, not sure I should speak to her of Mary Stuart, and annoyed with myself for having brought it up. But it was too late to retreat. "Your father's mother was attended by four women of the same name: Mary. But she lived in France for a long time, and so they were all called Marie."

She sat up and looked at me excitedly. "Mary Stuart, you mean?"

"Yes," I answered. "Your grandmother."

"Mary, Queen of Scots," she said, firmly and knowingly.

"Yes."

"She was a Catholic, wasn't she?"

"Yes. She was."

"And Queen Elizabeth cut off her head."

The frankness of the statement was abrasive. No one had ever described it so to me before. "Elizabeth, you shouldn't say it so —"

"She was trying to take Queen Elizabeth's throne, so she cut off her head. And Queen Elizabeth still feels badly about it, so she's going to leave her throne to my lord father when she dies. That's what you meant when you said we all may be moving before long. She's old, and isn't going to live much longer. And then we'll all move to England!"

Appalled, I'd heard enough. I stood her up before me and grasped both her hands. "Where did you hear all of this?"

She could see I was disturbed, and concern showed on her face. "My lady mother, I'm sorry —"

"No, my dear, you don't have to apologise. But you are talking of things that can be dangerous to talk about. Wherever did you learn of them?"

She looked confused. "Everyone talks of them," she offered timidly. "Often."

Her reply was nothing short of astonishing; at court, no one spoke of Mary Stuart. The household she was in was a Catholic one, and I immediately suspected that what she'd heard had been biased in Mary Stuart's favour. "Whose side do they take," I asked slowly, "Queen Elizabeth's, or Queen Mary's?"

"Some like one, some the other. Some say Elizabeth was right to kill her, that she deserved it, but others say not." She leaned in slyly and said, "But when I play with the other children there, and we pretend we're them, I always choose to be Queen Elizabeth. We've the same name, haven't we? But I like being her best because she won the fight. But please, you mustn't tell my lord father. He might not like it, since it was his mother who was killed."

The thought of my daughter playing at what had been a tragedy was shocking, and for a moment I couldn't speak. But then I grasped how fortunate it was that she'd told me, for I could now set a course that would keep her from harm. There were too many people who would seek to use her for their own political purposes, and even at so young an age she needed to learn to be careful.

"Elizabeth," I said with deep seriousness. "You must listen to me closely, and pay careful attention to what I have to tell you. What happened between your grandmother and your cousin was very, very sad, and is something many people still have strong feelings about. It has never been determined what the truth of so much of it was. Queen Elizabeth has always said the kill — the execution, was a mistake. This is not for you to be talking about with anyone, let alone making a game out of. Many people don't agree about things to do with religion; the Calvinists — which we are — are on one side, and the Catholics on the other. In this matter, for long and complicated reasons, the Calvinists take Queen Elizabeth's side, and the Catholics, Mary Stuart's. But you, my daughter, must take neither. Even if you are asked directly about it, you must say it is something you know nothing about. Elizabeth, you must heed what I tell you. It could be dangerous for you not to, dangerous not only for you, but for all of us."

She'd been staring at me as though fascinated. Finishing, I was prepared for some intense response, a display of fear, perhaps, now that the dangers had been made clear. But instead, she simply said, "Yes, my lady mother." Then she yawned and asked if she could take her new dress back to Linlithgow with her. When I replied that of course she could, she asked if I could have velvet in different colours sent afterward, so she could have more of the same style made. And as I tucked her into bed, she once again lamented not being able to shop in Edinburgh before leaving.

Henry was already in his nightshirt and robe when I entered his room, seated at a table by the fireplace beside the Earl of Mar. Both stood and bowed. "Leave us," I said coldly to the earl, who silently bowed again and went out.

Alone, I looked down at my son, and felt the wave of love and deep pride I always did when I first came into his presence, even after the briefest of absences. The accomplishment of my life had been to give birth to such a child, who in every way had fulfilled my hopes and expectations. His resembling me so closely in appearance, in the shape of his face and body, and colouring, and the fluidity of his movements, had only deepened my satisfaction. His interests also were much like mine. He was no intellectual, as James was, instead preferring more dynamic pursuits, and he excelled at games and exercise, and dancing, and could already play a number of musical instruments. He rode perfectly and kept numerous pet dogs, all of whom adored him.

The open book on the table was the Bible, which apparently he'd been reading aloud from before I came in. He'd also done well at his studies, although he would never be renowned for his scholarship. Complexities of thought bored him, as though he found them irrelevant, and in this we were also much the same. As I sat down at the table where the earl had been, I thought there could be few things so gratifying as to see oneself in a child. In some ways, it even made up for James's having separated us, for had I been present daily to influence his development, we could not have been more similar.

He stood waiting for me to tell him to sit also, which I did with a flick of my hand. Then I pointed to the Bible. "You were reading aloud?"

"We do every night."

The pages were parted early. "The Book of Exodus?" I guessed.

"Yes. Tonight, the earl chose the story. It was about Moses and the parting of the Red Sea. Mostly when he chooses, it's from the New Testament. But I like the Old Testament much better. The story of Moses is one of my favourites."

It was no surprise that the Old Testament appealed to him, with its tales of great leaders and warriors and kings, all very dramatic and colourful and adventurous. He went on, "Moses led his people to a new land. The earl says my lord father is to lead us to a new one also. He said he doesn't believe in signs, but if he did, the first-footer being English would be one."

I hesitated, because it wasn't wise to discuss our expectations of the English throne too much, particularly with him. Elizabeth had mentioned it also, but there was more danger in others trying to manipulate Henry politically. Although there was little I liked about the Earl of Mar, he was known for prudence, and his remark was unusual. "Why did he say that?" I asked casually, pretending indifference.

"Because I asked him why everyone had applauded the first-footer being English."

"What else did he say?"

"That the time of the Promised Land is approaching."

"Did he explain what he meant?" I well understood the earl's meaning, but I wanted to see how much Henry did.

"No. But he didn't have to. He meant that Queen Elizabeth should soon die, and leave her throne to my lord father."

"The earl believes the Promised Land is England?"

Henry became very still in his chair, and his face took on a look of the utmost gravity, unexpected in one so young. In a tone approaching reverence, he answered, "He says the Promised Land will be a new one, made up of both England

and Scotland. They are now two countries, but my lord father is going to join them as one. It is to be a Godly land, an example for all of Europe."

As though thinking aloud, I said slowly, "And so that is why he chose the story of Moses tonight. The earl believes James is chosen by God to lead us to a new Promised Land."

Henry's already extremely serious look deepened even further. "And if he fails, I am to do it."

Once, long ago, right after Henry's birth, I'd seen the look of an old man come over James. It had passed quickly, but had been unsettling, and I hadn't forgotten it. In other rare moments, I'd caught shades of it again, but as James had physically begun to age, it had then seemed less strange, and I'd barely thought of it at all. But now I saw something similar come over my child; he suddenly looked as if his youth had been stolen.

Henry had turned to the open Bible on the table, but at that moment he looked back at me. Those beautiful eyes, perfectly shaped and of a shade of blue identical to mine, looked cold and empty, devoid of his usual exuberance. In a small voice that sounded more confused than anything else, he said, "But I don't think I know how to do that."

I flung my arms wide, indicating he should come to me. He did so immediately, and I grasped him tightly, saying, "These are not concerns for a child, even a prince! Don't look so troubled!"

"Moses failed to enter the Promised Land," he whispered. "If Father fails, then I must be the leader." His tone was thin, but his fears were as loud as if he'd screamed them. From the way I was holding him, I couldn't see his face, which I was thankful for. If I saw a look there to match his voice, it might be too much for me.

With deep feeling, I said, "Moses failed because he doubted. Do you remember the story? He hit the rock twice with the stick. But your father never doubts anything!" A short, abrupt laugh escaped from my lips. "Even when his decisions are wrong."

I had more angry things to say, but I stopped; it wouldn't do to have Henry more troubled. It was unusual that he'd expressed fears to me at all, probably only because it was so late at night after the strangeness of the Hogmanay celebration, and weariness had caused him to speak more freely. It would only disturb him further to hear me criticise his father, or even his guardian. What I needed to do was restore his confidence, let him know his abilities were such that he would capably handle whatever life asked of him — as king.

Gently, I released him, indicating he should take his chair again. I half expected to see tears on his face, but to my relief, there were none. Even while acknowledging doubts and fears, he had retained his composure. And the look of the weary old man was gone.

"Henry," I said when he was seated, "as king, your father does as he sees fit to do. But when you are king — after him — those choices are to be your own. No matter what anyone else expects of you."

"The earl says my lord father is directed by God."

"God may direct you differently," I said reassuringly. "But I don't think that is something you should say to either the earl, or your father. Or anyone — except me, of course. I am so proud of you, Henry. Everyone is. You're going to make a wonderful king someday."

His smile showed how much the praise pleased him, but with it was a touch of surprise, as though he was reluctant to believe it. I felt the familiar resentment towards James for having prevented me from being present enough in his life to routinely offer encouragement. But at least I could see that I'd in so short a time made an impression on the child, and I was grateful the opportunity had arisen for me to do so. And grudgingly, I still had to acknowledge that he hadn't been neglected. In almost every other way, Henry was the very model of the perfect prince.

"Where are the toy soldiers I gave you for Hogmanay? I hope you like them? I had them specially made for you."

"Very much!" He jumped up and went to get them. I closed the Bible and pushed it to one side. There was much beauty and wisdom in both the Old Testament and the New, but one had to be careful that things in it weren't taken the wrong way.

Henry returned and arranged the soldiers in a straight line. "When I'm grown," he said, "I'm going to lead a great army, the best the world has ever seen. And a navy, too. I'm going to send ships to America, and start colonies there, and I won't let the Spanish take them from us."

He said it with such strength, it was as though he was seeing that new world across the ocean. No one yet knew the extent of it, except that it was vast. "But the Spanish are already there," I cautioned. "They have the advantage."

"Only in the south," he answered, with excitement. "There are more lands in the north. Queen Elizabeth tried to start a colony in Virginia, which failed. But I'm not going to fail! My lady mother, when we move to England, can I have a ship to go and start another? It's what I most want to do, something important that everyone remembers me for. Suppose I found a passage to the Orient?"

His face was an eight-year-old's, but his words were those of an ambitious adult. He wanted the English throne as much as James and I did, but even at so young an age, he had reasons of his own. He had dreams of exploration and adventures and renown. He'd learned that the English were explorers but the Scots weren't, and our moving to England would bring him one step closer to achieving his goals. His asking for a ship when we moved there was far from an idle request.

But he would never, as a prince and heir to the throne, be able to make so dangerous a voyage. A leader of a great army, or even a navy, was a possibility for him, because the peaceful Europe James longed for might never exist. But a perilous journey of exploration would be out of the question.

I tried a gentle discouragement: "Magellan already found the passage. And the English Drake sailed all the way around the world."

Scowling, Henry leaned forward, and with a finger knocked over one of the soldiers. "Drake was a pirate," he said dismissively. "And although Magellan found one southern passage into the far ocean, it's said there's another! Magellan may not be the only one people are going to say was a great discoverer." He flicked over a second soldier. "There may be another passage, in the north." His eyes widened. "One yet to be discovered, a faster one, far away from the Spanish ports. If we found it, we could take the orient trade from the Spanish. And that would be something for any king to be proud of!"

"It would," I agreed, my hesitation dwindling beside the sheer ambition of his plans. "But haven't others already tried?"

"Cabot, Frobisher, Gilbert, and Davis," he recited, counting off each name on his fingers. "The English have long wanted to find it. Cabot sailed for King Henry VIII."

"But if none of them succeeded, doesn't that mean there isn't one?"

"No." He turned to me with a distant look; he was clearly envisioning that northern passage. Slowly and convincingly, he said, "It means, my lady mother, that they looked in the wrong places."

And to the simple good sense of that answer, I could make no reply.

11

When the door to Henry's room had finally closed behind me, I was tired and ready to retire; Charles would be asleep and unaware whether I visited him or not. My gentlewomen, clustered in the corridor on little stools the valets had brought for them, looked as though they could fall asleep where they sat. But it was my responsibility to see my youngest child, so I started off in the direction of his room rather than my own.

His nurse, a robust and cheerful middle-aged woman, well-dressed but still with the look of a sturdy farmer's wife, was sitting beside his cradle, ready to begin rocking at his slightest stirring. She stood and curtsied as soon as she saw me. "We've usually a rocking woman all night, in case he wakes," she said quietly. "But tonight, I knew you'd come, no matter how late. So, I stayed with the duke."

An uncomfortable feeling of maternal inadequacy tugged at me, for having even momentarily considered not making the visit. The room was lit only by the light from the fireplace, and I was relieved that my expression wouldn't be clear in the dimness. "You wanted to speak to me?"

"Yes, about his cradle here."

It was still the same one he'd used at birth, for although he'd recently passed his second birthday, he was small. Unlike his brother, he'd been sickly, and was growing slowly. He also had yet to walk alone, or speak an intelligible word.

She said, "Next time we come here, he will need a larger one. He barely fits in this anymore. At Dunfermline we've moved him into a larger one."

Surprised, I looked down at his sleeping form, and saw that indeed he had grown — a little. It had been hard to tell earlier when I'd seen and held him upon arrival, and later during the celebrations. But again, I felt deficient for not having noticed. "Yes, he's grown," I replied.

Tactfully, the nurse said, "I wrote to you about this, Your Grace. Perhaps you didn't get the letter?"

With effort, I vaguely remembered one of my secretaries showing one to me, and having put it aside for response. "Yes, I received it. I'm afraid it was overlooked. In the future I'll be sure to pay closer attention, and reply promptly." I'd encouraged the everyday attendants of the children to approach me directly regarding anything of concern. The formal communications of the different earls and countesses who were their guardians were accurate, but the process was always lengthy and awkward, and sometimes with political tones. Hearing from those directly involved with the children's care was quicker and more reliable. It was important that I in no way now gave the impression of not caring, for the woman would then be reluctant to approach me again, possibly for a more serious problem. I reached over and lightly touched her arm, strong-feeling beneath the soft velvet sleeve. "It gratifies me to know someone so vigilant has the care of my child."

The touch was effective, as it always was, an enhancement of spoken praise. She smiled broadly, and said, "It's an honour to do so. I care for him as though he were my own."

Unexpectedly, Henry's ambition to lead expeditions leaped into my thoughts, and the futility of his ever fulfilling his dream because he was a prince. *Charles might indeed have a more fulfilling life if he'd been born to this woman instead of me.*

Quickly, I pushed the thought away, attributing it to the lateness of the hour. I asked, "I assume he hasn't walked yet?"

"He has — but not alone. And he can stand, holding onto something."

"Yes, you wrote me that." I smiled apologetically. "That was one letter I didn't overlook. No words yet?"

"Nothing distinct." Encouragingly, she added, "But I'm sure he understands much of what is said to him."

Suddenly, I said, "He is slower than his siblings were." Usually I was careful not to express worries, but I was tired, and it had simply slipped out.

But the woman's immediate response was full of hope and determination. "All children are different, Your Grace. I've five of my own, and none were the same, some fast and eager to take their place in the world, and others slower, more cautious. But in the end, all grew up fine."

My hand, still on her arm, instinctively tightened; I was grateful not just for what she said, but for her presence in Charles's life. I looked down into the cradle, where he was sleeping soundly on his back, the embroidered blanket pulled up to his chin, his little head covered by a perfectly white linen cap. One of his arms had reached out over the blanket, the fingers looking impossibly small and delicate. Even though he looked larger than I remembered, he still seemed so very fragile, in ways neither Henry nor Elizabeth ever had. For an instant, I wanted to pick him up and hold him in my arms, as if I could pour my own strength and vitality into him. But I knew I shouldn't, for if awakened from a sound sleep, he would cry, and I knew his crying fits had always been difficult to soothe.

The woman must have sensed my feelings, for she said, "The doctors all say he is progressing satisfactorily. He is becoming stronger. Were he not, he would not have made this trip to court for Hogmanay. It is a good sign, Your Grace."

All at once, a great tension eased out of me. It was difficult for me to acknowledge that I felt differently about this child than I did about my others. I loved him, but not with the same forceful attachment. Because of his sickliness, I'd always had worries I'd never experienced with Henry or Elizabeth, fears that had been aggravated by the loss of two other children. His greater needs had also made the separation from him even more difficult to bear. My feeling of powerlessness had at times been almost impossible to tolerate, and I'd responded by avoiding thinking of him. I disliked myself for doing so, but although I felt inadequate, it was a way of keeping my worries and fears in check.

It was some consolation to know there were others who were attending him to the best of their abilities, others such as this good woman standing beside me, with her clear devotion to him. It was absolutely essential that I maintain it, not only for Charles but for my own peace of mind. Letting go of her arm, I pulled a ring from my finger, one with several small diamonds set in gold, and pressed it into her palm. "A gift," I said quietly. "But not merely for Hogmanay. It is to show how much I value you. Please, take care of this child. For I cannot be there to do so myself."

She looked down at it, astonishment showing on her face, soon followed by pride. I could tell she'd responded to it as more than a mere payment; it was a token of the trust she'd earned, the trust of a queen. I then left the room, quietly so as to not wake my sleeping child. For all my weariness I felt satisfaction that much had been accomplished, much that I hadn't understood I'd wanted before entering, which was ensuring Charles's care, and reassuring myself I loved him.

It was very late, but one of James's attendants was waiting in the corridor outside my room. He whispered to Anna, who then said, "The king wishes to come to your room tonight." I replied that he should so directly, before I was in bed. It was time to tell him I was with child again. The good news would make up for the knowledge that for many months ahead he wouldn't be sharing my bed at night.

Before he arrived, I had Anna send the other women to bed, saying she would be sufficient to attend me after the king had left. When they were gone, I said to her, "Your remark at the celebration about Hogmanay being pagan was not only awkward, but dangerous. What is wrong with you to have said such a thing? You know how hard my husband has worked to maintain the religious balance in this country. I don't care to what extent you favour the Catholics, or if you've even become one yourself. But you must be careful, for my sake. People know our closeness, that we are almost sisters. Your opinions will be interpreted as mine!"

"You miss the twelve days of Christmas," she said. "I know you do."

Her behaviour had changed over the years, becoming more mysterious. She often answered even the simplest questions evasively. Whatever her reasons, it was clear to me she enjoyed it, and so I tolerated it, and was often amused. But tonight, I was not having it. "Yes, I do. And I believe it wise for the Lutherans to allow the celebrations. I don't believe the old Catholic rituals — even the Mass — cause harm, as the Calvinists do. But we live in a time where there is much disagreement in these matters. If out of nothing more than respect for the opinions of others, I cannot seem supportive of anyone who makes a provocative remark such as you did tonight. Be careful, Anna. Fortunately, what you said was quickly overlooked."

"I'm sorry for having disturbed you. It was not my intent."

But harsher words were needed, ones that were even a little cruel. Carefully, and very precisely, I said, "Did you think yourself of such importance that your religious opinion would make any difference whatsoever to anyone there? To these people who have nearly destroyed their country with their divisions over religion? For you can believe me, it did not. The most erudite minds in this land have failed to persuade, yet you flattered yourself you would succeed. Take care also, Anna, that you do not become a source of ridicule for everyone."

She'd seemed to dwindle in size as I'd spoken, some spirit or inner support draining away. What I'd said had been effective, but I immediately regretted having hurt her. "Anna," I began. But she stopped me by lifting her hand, as though to block whatever I had to say. She looked directly at me, and her expression said what her lips would not, that I had everything and she had nothing, now that I had taken the last crumb from her.

I went to her and grabbed both of her hands, interlocking her fingers with my own. "Believe that I need you here with me," I said. "Believe that you are the reminder for me of who I am beneath being queen. Believe that my family needs you also, and that this country needs us. Find satisfaction in that. And then if your Catholic sympathies give you comfort, take it. But do not forget us."

She closed her eyes for the briefest of moments, and when she reopened them, I saw my words had been effective. "I did forget," she said. "But only for a little while."

James's arrival prevented any further discussion, and Anna curtsied low to him and bowed her head as she hurried out. He had a tentative air about him, uncertain if my not wanting him to spend the night meant I was angry, or ill, or simply tired. The occasions when I didn't welcome him to my bed were few and far between. It flattered me that he still found me desirable, and I liked his visits, especially those where he stayed the entire night, for being queen could be lonely, and more than with anyone else I felt he could sympathise with me — but not completely.

His clothes were the same he'd worn earlier, since he'd not yet returned to his rooms, being occupied with the nobles who'd come for Hogmanay. Yet despite the lateness he still looked unrumpled in his embroidered white satin doublet and trunks, wide lace collar, and rich red velvet cloak, bordered with pearls. Even without his crown he looked as regal as he had earlier, when we'd stood with our children at the window for the crowd to see.

"I am with child," I told him at once. "Three of my courses have been missed."

He smiled widely, but not with complete surprise. "Your message gave me hope of it." Suggestively, he said, "Perhaps we should expect an English child."

I gave a little laugh. "Your good cousin Elizabeth is blessed with longevity."

"The first-footer was English." Light-heartedly, he added, "If we are to pay attention to omens."

"Born here or in England, I hope only for a strong and healthy child. Praise God that Charles finally seems to thrive." I went to the fireplace, where one chair had already been set in readiness for me, and pulled up another next to it. "Here, sit beside me for a while. It's so late already, it won't matter if we stay up a little longer. I want to tell you of my visit just now with our children. Especially, Henry."

"Henry," he repeated thoughtfully, as he came across the room with a steady and sure step, sturdier than it had been when he was younger. His awkward movements had smoothed out over the years, and he was often stiller, and in repose.

Seated on the two cushioned chairs, we could have been any husband and wife before a cosy fire on a cold winter night, with our children soundly tucked into bed. How would it be if we weren't the royal family, and were living without such great pressures and tensions, where so much was always at stake? But we were who we were, and it was foolish to think that anyone's life would be free of problems.

I said, "Charles grows, and is stronger. I didn't notice it when he arrived, but it was clear when I saw him in his cradle. He barely fits in it anymore. Elizabeth progresses nicely also, although her main concern appears to be her wardrobe. And Henry is becoming ambitious."

James looked startled, causing me to think I'd somehow said the wrong thing. Then he leaned back and folded his hands together, resting his elbows on the chair arms. "Tell me more," he said with quiet focus. "About Henry."

"He hopes to be an explorer of the new lands across the Atlantic."

James relaxed. "Oh, that is all," he said, with a small but unmistakable note of relief that confused me. But before I could question it, amusement showed on his face, a slight smile appearing on his lips as he said, "He's never told me that." Then he laughed fondly. "That is not going to happen."

I felt a little sad, as though I'd seen something destroyed, tossed into the fire or thrown down and stepped on. "I know," I said wistfully. "But it was so charming to listen to him. He has dreams of finding a northern passage to the Orient, and surpassing the Spanish."

"He has never told me of them. Not once, during any of my visits." There was unexpected resentment in his voice. James, as a matter of state and to supervise his education, visited Henry every month. Surely there was much they spoke of he never reported to me, and it seemed petty for him to be troubled by something our son had shared with me but not him.

I continued, "He's made a great study of it, apparently. He knows all about Virginia, and the settlement that failed there, and who the English explorers were, back to Cabot. He has great admiration for the English, and their endeavours. More than anything, he is eager to move to England to facilitate more of them."

While speaking I'd faced James directly, almost challengingly, as if trying to salvage some portion of Henry's impossible ambition. Briefly, I thought of saying more — how he also wanted to lead armies, a goal that wasn't so impossible. But James wouldn't respond favourably, since it didn't fit with his own desires for European peace. And although I felt I was no longer fighting for myself, but for Henry, I had no desire to provoke an argument.

James's attitude, though, suddenly changed for the better. "My son," he said supportively, "will be able to direct expeditions while not participating himself. And isn't that greater involvement, to sponsor and plan such enterprises? I must send him books about the great Portuguese prince, Henry the Navigator, whose work is unsurpassed. It may encourage him that his mother was an English princess, a Plantagenet, a daughter of John of Gaunt. And then, of course, there is the name, Henry." He leaned back in his chair and touched his beard. "But you understand he'll never be able to go himself, don't you?"

"Of course. When he told me, he tried to deflect it, but I wasn't able to as skilfully present a reason as you have now."

"It's the type of thing he's sure to understand himself as he grows and sees his responsibilities. I've been preparing a book for him about many things he needs to learn, directed toward him, specifically. I intend it to be the book he relies on above all others. Except the Bible."

"He was reading from it when I came in." I smiled, remembering. "He prefers the Old Testament."

A moment passed, during which there was only the sound of the fire crackling, and the wind outside. "The weather has changed," I commented, looking toward the window. "It was calmer at midnight."

James turned his head slightly toward the window, then back to me. "Henry — and Charles later — need to pay attention to the stories of the brothers in the Old Testament. We need to foster accord between them, not rivalry. The religious quarrels of our time would make them easy prey for those who would advance their own plans. I will instruct Mar to direct Henry to them."

As always, I disliked even the mention of Henry's guardian, but I couldn't argue with the wisdom of what James was suggesting. He went on, "Henry now thinks sailing across an ocean and discovering new things about the earth would be a spectacular way to spend one's life. But the true accomplishment would be the successful ruling of this island of two joined nations. More than anything else, we must teach him that."

Suppose he didn't want to? I wouldn't allow the thought to linger. James was right; I needed to gently encourage Henry to follow in his father's footsteps, to see that there were different challenges he would find as engaging as anything overseas or on a battlefield. To accomplish this, James and I needed to stand together, united.

The hour was late, and we both had responsibilities in the morning. I started to stand, but he stopped me with a single word. "Anna," he said.

There was no point trying to pretend I didn't understand him. I sighed and said, "Yes, I thought you would mention her. I've already spoken to her, seriously, about her comment tonight." I paused. "I spoke more harshly to her than ever before. She understood."

"Has she become a Catholic?"

"I don't think so. But I haven't asked directly. Some things it's better not to know the answer to."

"Others have noticed. They have asked me."

I waited a long moment before answering. "Tell them the queen tends to her own matters — all of them."

He didn't reply. For several moments we sat in silence, listening to the sound of the wind at the window. Finally, James said, "Hogmanay. Another one." And I wondered if next year we'd be celebrating Christmas instead.

12

During January there was nothing to suggest we'd be anywhere other than Edinburgh by the end of the year. Reports were that Queen Elizabeth continued as strong and hearty as ever, her vitality during the Christmas festivities lasting into the short winter days of the new year. In February, we heard that various ambassadors were received by her in splendid finery, and our gift of the elaborate cloak with the bird and flower design had been worn, along with other newly received gifts that had delighted her. James, who occasionally humoured my fondness of fine apparel by describing mentions of hers in letters he received, told me the Venetian ambassador had been particularly impressed by her appearance in a splendid gown of silver and white taffeta, trimmed with enormous numbers of pearls and diamonds. Elizabeth's wardrobe and jewels would be a comparably insignificant part of our English inheritance, but I couldn't deny it was pleasing to think they'd eventually be mine. Meanwhile, I found it curiously satisfying to know she still wore them to such great effect after so many years. From the news we'd been receiving, she might very well go on doing so for a number of months, if not years to come. The child I was expecting in June — who quickened as expected at the beginning of February — might be born in Scotland after all.

But at the beginning of March there was a change. Letters to James began to tell of a pervasive melancholy that had taken hold of the queen, which she wasn't able to overcome. "Her gloom is now apparent to all," he said. "But no one can tell the cause of it, and she refuses to answer probing questions. She has said only that she isn't well, although she appears to be —

in body. Something seems to weigh on her spirit, although her court is mystified as to what could be troubling her."

We were at dinner when he told me this, and I was quickly distracted from dwelling upon the news. But on my way back to my rooms I passed the window where we'd stood during Hogmanay, and I remembered the first-footer had been English. The change for which we'd hoped and waited so patiently might finally be at hand. I paused at the window and looked out at the now nearly empty expanse in front of the palace, and the city rooftops and church spires beyond the gates. It seemed almost impossible that we would leave Edinburgh for good. A wave of excitement passed through me, so intense it left me breathless. With it came a new anxiety; to rule one country was nearly impossible, even when one had, like James, been doing so nearly from birth. Would it be possible to rule two with success?

I must have swayed a little, for behind me one of my gentlewomen asked with concern, "Your Grace, are you well?"

One of my hands fluttered out to touch the side of the window. I drew a steadying breath, and replied that I was fine. Beneath my fingertips the very walls of Holyrood Palace felt reassuring, a reminder that years of experience would assist with the magnitude of the change and tasks ahead. As I moved away from the window, sure of my step again, I told myself it was premature to speculate on what the days ahead would bring. It was entirely possible that Queen Elizabeth would emerge from her melancholy, and continue ruling for years.

Two weeks later it was evident she would not and that her decline would be fatal. The news was that she had retired to her rooms at Richmond Palace, where melancholy had deepened into apathy and lethargy, and she refused all medical care. She sat endlessly on cushions on the floor, neither moving nor speaking, staring at nothing, her gentlewomen and courtiers hovering at a distance. The sadness of her being alone at such a time, without children or a husband, much affected me. My own loneliness and isolation as queen had been difficult enough, but certainly hers had been harder. Yet there had been choices involved. Despite the struggles and worries of marriage and children, magnified and compounded for anyone who sat on a throne, was it not better than having lived one's life alone?

The letters to James now consistently told of his succession being openly spoken of and expected by many, and he was even sent for approval a draft of the English Councillors' proclamation of him as king to be read when the time arrived. "Above all else, I desire a peaceful transition," James said to me. "And I hope this doesn't drag on for too long. For Elizabeth's sake, mostly — a quick death is always a gift from God. But for my sake as well. In the haze of a vague waiting period, who knows what dissent might arise?"

We were alone in his rooms, where he'd called me to discuss the most recent news. The anticipatory tension of the last weeks had drawn us even closer than the pursuit of the common goal had for so many years. It was something we shared with no one else, and it bonded us. I said encouragingly, "There hasn't been any other candidate for years. Assembling support for one isn't easy, and takes time."

But James was unwilling to so easily agree. "There is always someone keenly alert, waiting to seize an opportunity. Discord could come not only from the Catholics, but the more radical of the English reformers, the Puritans. I have carefully laboured to present us as moderate in our beliefs and respectful of those of others. The Calvinism we've practised here is closest to the Puritans, but I've continued to favour some Catholics, which shows an intent to pursue the middle Anglican course. We are acceptable to all sides, and feared by none — now. But the current situation creates a void, which could disrupt this balance."

"It's not likely, though, is it?"

"No. The most powerful lords in England — and the richest, with the most followers — approve of me. Of us — all of us, including the children. They feel the appearance of a royal family after nearly half a century of an unmarried queen will make an enormous impression on the English populace. Especially since two of the children are named Henry and Elizabeth."

The very air between us had seemed to crackle with the tension of our concerns as he'd spoken. He'd been gripping the arms of his chair, but now he let go and said more softly, "I also would very much like our child to be born in England."

"I expect to be delivered in June. I can safely travel through the middle of May."

His face took on a gentler look. "You continue in good health?"

I lightly touched my midsection. "My physicians are well satisfied."

"The English climate is milder than here in Scotland. It should be easier for the new infant to thrive than it was for Margaret or Robert."

His mention of them, even to me, was rare. Sometimes I'd wondered if he'd felt their loss as keenly as I had. Now I knew he had. I went and stood behind him and placed my hands on his shoulders, which beneath the soft velvet of his tunic felt tense and tight. For all his control of demeanour, the strain of waiting was affecting him. I said, "It's one more way England should be good for us. There may be greater medical knowledge, along with more money for care. Here, we are rich, by Scottish standards, and all our children have been given the best care possible. But England is a land of much greater wealth and resources. Our children are going to have even better lives than they've had here."

James reached up and grasped one of my hands, and for a long moment we remained so, finding unspoken comfort and reassurance in each other. Then we were interrupted by a knock on the door, sudden and jarring. James was needed for consultation with his stewards.

For the next few days I with effort kept my thoughts on routine matters, but they were interspersed with moments of nearly unbearable tension, and others of excited anticipation. Every courier arriving at the palace, any attendant appearing unexpectedly, was cause for speculation that they might bear the awaited news. My admiration for James's apparent self-control deepened, and I took it as standard for my own. The knowledge that all eyes in the palace were watching us, to which I was usually indifferent from long familiarity, suddenly held a new cruelty. Even the causal glances from my gentlewomen felt prying. Night, when the curtains of my bed were closed around me, felt a blessed relief.

Finally, one night near the end of the month, I awoke from a deep sleep to find the curtains pulled back and all the candles in the room lit. James was standing at the foot of the bed in his nightshirt and a heavy robe, gazing down at me. I felt at once it wasn't morning, or close to it, and that I hadn't been asleep for long. Immediately, even before I had fully thrown off sleep, I knew the long-awaited event had happened.

James looked as though he'd been standing there for some time, waiting for me to wake. Seeing that I had, he said quietly, "I am King of England."

I pulled myself up, propping the pillows behind me. Queen Elizabeth was dead. James was King of England. And I was queen of another country. Strangely, I felt no thrill or satisfaction. To my complete surprise, I felt only relief. I held back a great desire to lie down and go back to sleep. But then, a deep and powerful interest in observing James grasped me, as though it were of vital importance for me to fully understand his response. I looked at him questioningly.

He continued, "Two days ago, Queen Elizabeth died. I was proclaimed King of England from the gates of Westminster Palace." His voice was very soft, but the words were clear. "All the church bells in London rang. There were celebratory bonfires throughout the city."

His eyes were still turned towards me, but clearly saw much more. I waited. Waiting was something I had learned how to do well.

He then gave a deep sigh, his shoulders heaving, as though the weight of a lifetime was being released. Then he appeared to be drawn back to me. "Anne," he said, a fond smile briefly drifting across his face, "word arrived shortly after we retired." He paused. "The report of Elizabeth's final days was thorough. God was merciful, and did not allow her to linger. After days in her torpor on the floor, she finally agreed to take to her bed. There, attended by praying clergy, she passed in and out of consciousness. The prayers seemed to comfort her."

He tilted his head upward, looking above me as his mood shifted again. Abruptly, his expression became completely blank. In a matching tone, except for the slightest trace of bitterness, he asked, "What did she think of during that time? During all those hours of melancholy while she sat on the floor? It's said she stuck her fingers in her mouth, like a child. What did she think of then, and later in her bed as her death approached?" His gaze lowered, fixing on my face, but the look was distant again, as it had been earlier. "Tell me," he went on with cold resentment. "Did she think of my mother, and wonder what her thoughts had been as her death had approached? My mother, whose death she ordered? Although she would never admit it." A single harsh laugh escaped from his lips. "Is that what the great Queen Elizabeth thought of in her last hours of life?" He looked down at the floor. Again, he sighed, but less heavily than before. He ran a hand through his hair, still as tousled as it was when he'd been awakened with the news. "It matters nothing now," he said gently, with resignation. "My mother murdered my father, and tried to murder Elizabeth. Desire for the English throne overwhelmed her. But my prudence has brought it to me where her ruthlessness did not. I am now King of England and Scotland. I am King of Great Britain."

Whatever internal shift had been needed for him to accommodate the arrival of the immense change had been successfully accomplished. Before my very eyes his conflicting loyalties had been resolved. He was King of England, and I was queen. But I was only so through him, and it was my place to acknowledge it. The moment had come for me to rise from the bed and bow before him. He was standing, unspeaking, looking down at me from the end of the bed. It was impossible to tell whether he expected it or not.

He came around to the side of the bed, leaned down and lightly brushed his lips against my forehead. "The night is cold," he said, drawing the covers further up about me. "Sleep now. Tomorrow begins a new world for us."

On a morning of brilliant early April sunshine and breezes that were still cold but with hints of spring, we said goodbye at the gate of Holyrood Palace, before the two hundred Scottish lords and gentlemen who would accompany James to England, and much of the population of Edinburgh, come to wish him farewell, crowded in the streets beyond. I would follow later, and Henry and Elizabeth, after he'd arrived in London and was sure of a peaceful welcome. Charles was to remain in his household in Scotland until we were more certain the journey wouldn't adversely affect his health.

Although James remained dry-eyed, I gave way to tears during our final embrace before he mounted his horse and rode off at the head of the retinue, looking more regal and full of authority than ever in his tall plumed and jewelled hat, and ermine-trimmed blue travelling cloak. I stood at the gate watching, my gentlewomen and the remaining court gathered behind me, many weeping also, as he grew smaller in the distance and finally vanished. And then I dried my tears and led everyone back into the palace.

As I passed the closed door to James's rooms, his absence felt noticeable. It was nonsense for me to feel so, for we'd been separated many times before, sometimes for equally long stretches during his travels to remote parts of Scotland. His now going into a different country shouldn't account for any significant feeling of difference. But for the first time since that night nearly two weeks earlier, when I'd awakened and heard his announcement that he was King of England, I felt something had not only been accomplished, but finished. The days between had been so busy, so crammed with receiving the congratulating swarm of Scottish nobles from all over the country, and the merchants and burghers of Edinburgh, and then attending to all the preparations for the change, it was as if there'd not been time to absorb it. But now, James's departure seemed to have created room for its impact to become apparent.

Now that our goal of so many years had been achieved, I wondered what would replace it, and if it would be sufficient to prevent our bond from unravelling. In England, there would undoubtedly be even more new challenges. There'd be different social and political standards we would both have to learn to navigate. It was possible new bonds would form between us. James had years ago told me of feeling inadequate for the sophisticated culture of England, but he was confident I'd fit in to the admiration of all. Much would also depend on how the English responded to us. For nearly half a century they'd had only one royal figure to rally around — but now there were five. Time would tell how that would play out for all of us.

When we reached my rooms, Anna asked if I would dine alone there now that the king was gone. "No," I answered. "In the banquet hall, as usual. But have the king's chair removed."

Two days later I received word that as planned, James had crossed the border into England. His reception at Berwick couldn't have been more welcoming, with many English nobles having made their way north to greet him. I handed the letter to one of my secretaries, then went to the window and looked out over the empty expanse between the palace and the front gate. James seemed to have gone very far away indeed.

Further reports over the following days were replete with details of magnificent feasts and receptions, in Newcastle, Durham and York, with more and more English nobles and gentlemen joining the retinue everywhere. But although James's presence seemed to expand with each step of his journey toward London, to me alone in Edinburgh he felt more and more distant. It was not something I found uncomfortable. In his absence, I was coming to feel more important. It took only a few days before sitting without him at the end of the crowded banquet hall didn't feel strange at all. The novelty of having significant news delivered directly to me, instead of relayed through him as it always had been, was satisfying.

At the beginning of May I received a letter from Henry at Stirling, the first I'd had from him since James had left. It was unusual in itself, since he didn't usually write to me, all his correspondence being with James, who then passed to each of us greetings and other news. When I finished reading it, I stood holding it tensely in one hand, and with the other I waved away the secretary ready to take it. "Nothing troubling, I hope?" asked Anna.

Her face was full of genuine concern. Despite recent moments of difficulty with her, she was still the only one I could completely trust. "Come," I told her, and led her into the small inner room off my bedroom. With the door closed, I said, "Henry asks me to visit him in place of James, who used to go every month. When I saw the letter, I was sure it would be about his instructions for travelling to England, but he doesn't mention them. His not doing so is telling — he would have said so if he'd had them. This may be his way of saying he is concerned. I believe he fears being left behind."

"Wasn't that decided before the king left? Charles would remain, but the rest of you would follow shortly?"

"It was. But he hasn't been told of any plans yet — as I have." My departure had been delayed until after Queen Elizabeth's funeral so that participating noblewomen could meet me at Berwick to accompany me to London. I was still waiting to learn the final date, which I knew wouldn't be far off because I was rapidly approaching the time my condition would prevent me from travelling, and James wanted the child born in England. But it was odd that Henry had yet to be told anything at all. "Something in England could have caused James to change his mind. Before he left there was some discussion about leaving Henry here to maintain our family's presence in Scotland. Of course, I objected to it. And James felt strongly that the English needed to see he already had an heir."

"Why not enquire if the Princess Elizabeth has received instructions yet? If so, you may be right, and the king has changed his mind."

"It would break Henry's heart," I said with deep feeling. "And mine as well. I've already endured an almost unbearable separation from my son, and James knows it. Surely he wouldn't hurt me so again."

"You have resentments," she cautioned.

"This is a new matter," I said assertively. "Long ago, I resigned myself to the necessity of the prince having been removed from my care. I struggled, but eventually saw James meant it for his protection, given the unruliness of the Scottish lords. But I still despise the Earl of Mar. His mother may rest in peace." The old countess had died earlier in the year. Henry was now supervised by the earl and his young wife. Although I'd prayed for the old woman's soul, I couldn't deny I was pleased she was now removed from Henry's life.

Anna's frowned deeply and her lips compressed as she thought. Then she said reflectively, "The prince is still young. This is a change that could intimidate the most courageous of fully-grown men. He's likely afflicted by anxieties. It's unfortunate the king didn't reassure him before he left."

I agreed, and James's actions now seemed callous and shallow. "He sent him a letter when departing, and read it to me before he did. It was perfectly written, showing all his facility with language, and full of good advice warning Henry against pride in his new advancement. He told him to remember he was a king's son already." With a touch of rueful bitterness, I added, "And he sent him a copy of a book he'd written as a guide for his life. *The Basilikon Doron*, he called it. In Greek, it means 'royal gift'." It was difficult to prevent disdain from entering my voice. "How very like James, to send our son a book when what he needed was a visit. But he wouldn't travel the fifteen miles, nor now keep him informed of his plans for him. I wonder what small comfort Henry found in that book. And I wonder not at all that he's requested me to visit. I should, I think, make the trip. I must at least now consider it."

Anna left, and as the other gentlewomen started to come in, I told them I wanted to be alone. They went out, but sent in servants to stoke up the fire and pull one of the chairs up close to it, for although it was May it was still cool. Cushions were brought to make the chair more comfortable, and a footstool for my feet. Given my advanced and very visible condition, lately even more effort than usual had been made in attending me.

After some time, I called for Anna again and asked her, "The Earl of Mar went with James to England, didn't he?"

"Yes." There was something more certain in her manner now. She too had given the matter thought.

"And you've heard nothing of his having returned?"

"No."

"Neither have I — which is good. I've decided, Anna, it's important for me to have the prince with me when I arrive in England."

"I'd assumed he'd travel with you," she said. "It may very well still be the king's intent."

"I'd thought so, but now I have my doubts. He should have received instructions by now. I'm concerned, not only for the prince's well-being, but because it's very important for the English to see him arrive at my side. The princess also, but especially the prince. I need to make as strong an impression as James did." I waited for her to offer objections, or to tell me I was wrong. But when she didn't, I went on, "These past few weeks have shown me how it would be were I a queen regnant born to reign, and not just a queen consort. Everyone treats you differently, not only the nobles and the court but the merchants and even the servants. In England they are used to that type of queen, and they will see me as less, unless I show them I am something equal to although different from the queen they had. I must show them I am the mother of a prince. For all her glory, Queen Elizabeth never produced a child to succeed her."

"It was God who guided her choice of successor," Anna said firmly. "If God now is guiding you to Stirling and taking the prince under your care, you should follow without hesitation. He may not want the prince brought into England by someone with strong Calvinist faith — like the Earl of Mar. And that could very well be what the king intends to do now. This delay may be for the earl to return to accompany the prince."

The very suggestion of it was upsetting. "James wouldn't allow that! He's been intent on presenting us as religious moderates. We are to assure the English we take the middle path."

"But who knows who may have influenced him in England?" she asked quietly. "You above all others should stand closest to him. It is your duty as his wife to help him remember. The prince arriving with you speaks of much more to the English than your importance. Do not fear that you seek only to allay your fears or satisfy your vanity." She paused. "And the king may not be telling you of his new plan so as to have you already in England where you cannot object."

"He wouldn't allow that," I repeated, but much less strongly than before. Although unlikely, I couldn't deny what she suggested was possible. Who knew how James had been influenced in England? If his great reception and the grandiose wealth of England had already altered him? By the time I arrived the jubilation would be over, the novelty of a new monarch, and a king, passed. The English were used to seeing a queen. But a queen accompanied by her children would certainly generate another wave of excitement. And only by having my son beside me would I be able to stand equal to James before our new subjects.

I stood up, feeling the child within me move as I did. "My son has requested me to visit him. We depart as soon as tomorrow, or the first day the weather holds fair. I'll send word ahead that for sentimental reasons I want to visit Stirling Castle once more before leaving for England. We say nothing of intending to take the prince when I leave. Who knows? Before then, there could still be instructions from James for him to accompany me."

13

When we arrived at Stirling Castle it was immediately apparent there would not be any instructions from James. As soon as I stepped out of my carriage, the young Countess of Mar told me that her husband was to return in the middle of the month. What Anna had suggested was correct; James intended the earl to bring Henry to England.

So disturbing was the news that it nearly overshadowed my joy at the sight of Henry waiting just beside the countess. In the five months since I'd seen him at Hogmanay, he'd grown noticeably taller, and even at age nine the image of the striking adult he would be was starting to emerge. There was no question my arriving in England with him at my side would make an enormous impression.

He stepped forward and bowed, removing his hat in a grand sweeping gesture. "My lady mother, your visit is most welcome!" The barely contained excitement in his tone was telling of the depth of his sincerity.

Dropping formalities, I bent down and embraced him tightly. "You see I came at once when you asked me to," I said quietly into his ear, so that no one else could hear. "Say nothing to anyone, but you will come with me to England."

One of his hands resting on my arm tightened, telling me I'd correctly estimated the extent of his fears of not being taken. For all James's wisdom, what a fool he'd been to be so indifferent to the fears and hopes of his son! I felt a nearly overwhelming desire to pull him back into the carriage I'd just emerged from and gallop away, all the way to the border. But I fought it back and released him. The satisfaction in his eyes and the broadness of his smile were almost sufficient reward for me already. But I had as yet no cause at all to feel satisfied, for there was much to be done, and done quickly, now that I knew of the earl's planned return. I told Henry to go about his usual activities, and I would join him later. He bowed again and strode away, followed by four other youngsters about his age, who had waited behind him.

The countess, who had years ago been one of my attendants, was hovering uncertainly beside me. When I asked who the other children were, she replied they were hers — and the earl's. "They are the prince's closest companions here," she said proudly. "The earl wishes them to be as close to him as he was to the king when growing up."

And to foster dependency on them as well. It was rapidly becoming clear that I should have continued over the years to attempt to remove Henry from the earl's care. It was not too late, though — if I could detach him as I was now planning.

Meanwhile, it was important to not give any sign to the countess that I was agitated or disturbed at all. I smiled at her as though well pleased, and said, "How fortunate the prince has been to have had such fine companionship." And then I said I was tired from the trip and wished to go at once to my rooms.

There, the memories of giving birth to Henry in them added greater urgency to my mission. I called for paper and pen, and immediately sat down and began to write to several of my most loyal supporters, the lords Hamilton, Glencairn, Orkney, Linlithgow and Elphinstone. Although some would surely guess at it, I refrained from telling them I wanted to take Henry to England, and said only that a matter had arisen regarding the prince and I needed their help at Stirling Castle. None were friends to the Earl of Mar, and would welcome the opportunity to finally diminish him. Some had even been willing to ride with me to the same castle many years ago, when with Chancellor Maitland I'd tried to regain control of my son. That plan had failed, but the present circumstances were vastly different, with James so far away and importantly occupied in England. This time, there was no obstacle to my success.

The sealed letters were given to various trusted servants who'd accompanied me, and dispatched with the additional message that the recipients were to come as hastily as possible. The messengers were also not to tell anyone of their destinations, nor of the contents of the letters, and to slip away as unobtrusively as possible. Only after they were gone did my thoughts return to Henry.

I found him in the garden, taking exercise on the bowling green with his companions, the earl's sons I'd seen earlier and some others. A few girls watched from the sides. All were finely if soberly dressed, showing they were the children of Calvinist nobles. When they saw me emerge onto the terrace, the game stopped, and all saluted me with low bows and curtsies. Henry seemed uncertain whether he should leave the game and come to me, but I waved for him to continue. As the playing resumed it looked to me like a miniature version of James and my court, although more boisterous and exuberant. With a touch of loss, it occurred to me that it had been years since James had participated in such light-hearted sports or amusements.

Henry had removed his hat — now held as if a great treasure by one of the girls on the side — and the brilliant late morning sunshine caused his fair hair to look even more golden. It was quickly apparent that he dominated all aspects of the game, and the accompanying socialising, not in an overbearing way, but as the natural centre about which everything revolved.

Unlike his father he moved with considerable agility and grace, playing the game deftly. He showed pride in his own successes — repeatedly he struck down all pins with a single toss — but still complimented his companions on theirs. The deference of the others was subtle, almost invisible unless one knew what to look for, as I did. Yet they played well too, without simply allowing him to win, as my women sometimes still did with me, making his superior ability even more meaningful. I did, though, notice a touch of coldness in him toward them, a noticeable reserve, especially when they spoke. In that, James surpassed him, as did I, for we were both skilled in conversation with our court. It was something that would have been different, if Henry had been in my care instead of that of the dour Earl of Mar, his silly wife and his stern mother. There was no question it was time for a change. When we went to England, the Earl of Mar and his family were best left behind in Scotland.

But over the next few days, as I waited apprehensively for the arrival of the lords I'd written to, I saw he'd been taught many other things very satisfactorily. He sat beside me at dinner and supper, exhibiting perfect manners and knowledge of protocol. His education had been good, and he already read and spoke French.

"No other languages?" I asked him, somewhat surprised.

"A little Italian. My tutor substituted it for Spanish, which I refused to learn. The French and Italians are papists, but not our enemies. We are at war with Spain."

There was a distinct thrill in his voice as he said it. We were sitting on the dais in the Great Hall at dinner, the room crowded, everyone below alternating between watching us and their food as they ate. Henry had spoken softly, barely moving his lips, as all royalty was taught to do to maintain privacy in so visible a setting. I was pleased he'd learned something so important for a future king, but at the same time his opinions displayed the Calvinist slant of his education. He despised the Catholics, and the English war with Spain appealed to him. James wouldn't like it, being ambitious to create lasting peace in Europe. How ironic it would be should his son mature into a warrior king instead of a pacifist, because of the education he'd been so adamant he receive under the supervision of the Earl of Mar. But I felt no satisfaction at the thought that it would serve James right for his stubbornness in removing Henry from my care. Instead, for the first time, the inconsistency of James's decision to do so seemed baffling and mysterious. I was certainly more even-handed in my approach to religion than the Earl of Mar, entirely aligned with James's own attitudes. If he'd wanted to leave a successor to carry out his personal goals of European peace, why had he allowed him to be educated from such a one-sided point of view? Had his concerns and fears of the vying Scottish nobility really caused him to make a decision contrary to his own most deeply valued ambitions?

Henry was politely refusing a particularly rich dish with an aromatic sauce that I had just been served. Seeing I'd noticed, he said, "Too much heavy food makes me sluggish for my afternoon sport. I must always do my best at them."

"At your studies also," I said. "Tell me, have you learned Latin and Greek?"

He wrinkled his nose distastefully. "Barely. They bore me. And why should anyone learn Latin these days? The Bible is in English now."

"But there are many fine books in ancient languages."

"Can you tell me the name of one, my lady mother?" There was slyness in his voice. His subtlety amused me; he knew I was no scholar like his father, and wanted me to sympathise with him. I did — very much so — but the great responsibilities ahead of him in life were always to be taken into account.

I replied prudently, "All kings must be well educated. You should apply yourself to your studies. And I assume you've read your father's book? *The Basilikon Doron*? He wrote it especially for you."

"How could I not? My father will surely question me about it. And so, I have prepared myself."

"But what of the content? The values it recommends, and the advice? What do you think of that?"

"It is a great preparation for me to be king," Henry answered flatly, as though the reply had already been practised, given to him by others who correctly estimated what response would, eventually, have to be given to James. The boredom showing on his face deterred me from further questions, as did the yawn that followed, politely covered by his hand. Besides, I would have no reply if he pointed out that my saying the book had been for him was wrong, and that James had written it as a display of his own scholarship.

After dinner he rode out from the castle with some of his companions, under the supervision of the young Lord Erskine, the earl's eldest son, from his first marriage. My advanced condition prevented me from joining them, for although I was still allowed to ride, I had to be careful. The entire term had gone smoothly, with all expectations at the various months successfully passed, but I had the long trip to London ahead of me, and needed to preserve my strength. Since coming to Stirling Castle, the child within me had been moving more, and at different times than in the past, which had mostly been in response to my having consumed different foods than usual.

During the nights, my sleep had been disturbed by the child's new restlessness. My anxiety over the upcoming removal of Henry no doubt was of some influence — how could the unborn child not sense my agitation? — but it would soon be over. And there might be benefit to the child also, sensing the extent to which its mother would go to protect her children.

Late in the afternoon, before supper, Henry joined me again, in my rooms. It was always one of my favourite times of the day, especially in spring when the daylight lasted longer and the windows could be left open to the dusk breezes, with their scent of newly bloomed foliage. "How was your ride?" I asked.

"Very fine," he answered. "John — Lord Erskine — took us further than before. So, we didn't hunt today. We wouldn't have had time to both ride further and hunt."

"Who decided?"

"I did. But I spoke to the others before I did, to learn their minds. I always enjoy myself more if all are agreeable to a choice I'm given. I also try to see what Lord Erskine would prefer, especially if he is in a bad humour."

"And was he in one today?"

Henry had been casually striding about the room as we spoke, while I sat before the open window. But now he came and rested against the windowsill, leaning his elbows on it. "He always is when his father is gone, and he needs to be the one in charge. He's not used to it yet. He's only eighteen." He gazed ahead of him absently. "But with the old countess, it was the opposite. She was always in a better humour when the earl was away." He turned around and looked out the window. "I am sorry she is dead."

The remark completely surprised me. I said, "When one dies, we should always be charitable and pray for them. But you don't have to like them, if you didn't when they were alive. I always found the countess disagreeable. I also resented her meddling, with her son, in the affairs of our family."

"She was often kind to me," Henry said, continuing to face the window. "She was different when we were alone, or with only a few attendants. Then, she wasn't quoting the Bible all the time, like she was angry or disappointed with everyone. She would be very nice." An odd silence followed, before he added, "Right before she died, she called me to her room and sent everyone else out. When they were gone, she said she was sorry."

"Sorry?" I asked, with incredulity. "Did she really apologise for her part in taking you from me?"

"No. Not that."

"For what, then? I don't understand, Henry."

"Neither did I. So, I asked what she meant." He turned and looked directly at me. "She said she was sorry I was going to have to be king."

Baffled, I stared at him. I felt I should be affronted, but couldn't tell precisely why. "Whatever did she mean by that?"

Henry shrugged lightly. "I don't know."

Beneath his air of indifference, he was watching me intently. What the old countess had said had confused and troubled him, and he was looking to me for an explanation. But it was one I could not yet give. Instead, I asked, "Had she ever said it before? It was a very strange thing to say."

"No. But one time she said she wished she hadn't been a countess."

If she hadn't been, she never would have been able to trouble my family so, I thought to myself. *We wouldn't even be having the present conversation. All of us would have been better off.* But it wasn't something I could say to Henry. The woman had been kind to him, he'd said. Trying to avoid showing the extent of my concern, I asked with forced mildness, "During that last visit, was that all she said? Was there anything else?"

"She said the apology might as well come from her, since no one else was going to give it."

I was aghast. It was almost unimaginable that any nine-year-old, even a prince, should have to contend with a woman on her deathbed telling him such disturbing nonsense. "Whatever did you say then?" I heard myself ask.

"Nothing. As soon as she said it, she rested back on her pillows, like she was relieved. She died almost right after that, but I'd already left the room. When I did, everyone in the corridor was looking at me curiously, and wanted to know what she'd said. But I didn't tell them. I haven't told anyone, except you, today."

Any confusion I'd felt over her meaning was suddenly obliterated by anger. Even on her deathbed, the countess should never had said something so melancholy and devoid of hope about his future to my son. My hands clenched into fists, but I relaxed them at once when I felt the child within me start to move about, and I placed my hand over it soothingly. A soft breeze from the window touched my face, and helped calm me as I breathed deeply of it. Any agitation sensed by the unborn child as well as the one before me would be harmful to them. But it was nearly beyond belief that the woman had said such a meaningless and cruel thing to Henry. Worse, I could see it had impacted him powerfully. It was essential that I do my best to counter it. I gave a light laugh and, smiling tolerantly, said in a dismissive way, "You must ignore what she said. When some people are close to death, they become deranged. It is a wonderful thing that you will be king one day."

A certain tension seemed to go out of him, and he stood less rigidly, his face relaxed. "My lady mother," he said, extending his hand. "May I take you downstairs to supper?" As I stood up, I felt the child inside me was quiet again; I'd succeeded in calming both of them. But more than ever, I knew I'd made the right decision in coming to Stirling, and in planning to take Henry away when I left.

After supper, I received word that the lords I'd written to had pledged their support to any cause I set them to, and were already on their way. In the morning, they would meet first in the town below and come together to the castle. I sent for the young countess and told her I would be leaving the next day. "The prince accompanies me when I depart. Please have him and his attendants ready with whatever should be needed, not only for the trip to Edinburgh, but to London shortly after that."

All the colour seemed to drain from her face. She stood uncertainly, biting her lower lip and clutching her hands together. I was ready to speak harshly if she dared oppose me. We stood facing each other, my colourfully dressed gentlewomen behind me, her soberly garbed ones behind her, all in complete silence, during which it seemed that all the tensions of Scotland were present in the room. Then she curtsied, and they retreated. "Lock the doors," I said. "Tell the guards to say we have all retired, if anyone else comes here tonight."

During the night I barely slept at all, due to the child's restlessness and my apprehensions about what the next day would bring. I'd calculated there was insufficient time for a letter to be sent to either the earl or James for instructions, and I was counting on my own authority not being challenged, especially with the support of the lords I'd summoned.

As I lay awake, staring into the darkness as the hours crept by, my thoughts repeatedly returned to the mysterious words of the old countess. Henry's greatest fortune had been to be born the son of a king, and heir to not one throne but two, and welcomed by both kingdoms. James, despite his insensitivities as a father, was ruling with great intelligence and skill, and would undoubtedly prepare a smooth succession for his heir. Henry had been born into a charmed life. It was inconceivable that anyone should need to apologise to him for it. Yet as much as I wanted to dismiss what the countess had said as the rantings of an embittered old woman, I could not. Perhaps later, when we were all comfortably settled in England, I'd be able to.

In the morning the perfectly clear sky heralded success for my plans. Yet almost immediately I saw they wouldn't be achieved without a struggle. No sooner was I dressed than I received a message from the countess, asking me to delay my departure until she'd received permission from her husband to release the prince into my care. "Tell her no, with my apologies," I answered. "As the king desires our expected child to be born in England, I must depart almost at once to be settled there for a safe delivery."

Within minutes, the same attendant returned, this time requesting that the prince remain at Stirling when I left. "No," was all I replied. We then left for the morning prayer service at the chapel. The countess saluted me formally there, but said nothing, although the strained look on her face told of her concerns, as did the alert and vigilant attitudes of the men of her household, all behind her stepson Lord Erskine. The young man looked stiff and formal, and full of self-importance. I'd seen him before, in passing, but for the first time I noticed his distinct resemblance to his father. But still, he looked very youthful and inexperienced, and would certainly be no match for the arriving lords.

When we returned to my rooms, Anna whispered, "The lords all marched up from the town while we were in the chapel. It looks like an entire army in front of the castle gates, and some are inside too, in the courtyard. Lord Erskine and the countess have the guards preventing them from coming further. He's angry they made it so far into the castle already. The outer gate guards were overcome — in the name of the queen, they said."

"Tell Lord Erskine and the countess that my guests should be brought to me in my Inner Hall. You are known as my closest attendant, so go yourself and conduct them here. Tell them I am fine and there is no cause for any weapon to be drawn in my defence, or the prince's. But for now, their men should remain where they are, both inside the castle and without."

As I waited on my chair of state in the Inner Hall, the 'Hunt of the Unicorn' tapestries were a reminder of my unique and strange status. It was time for all to see I was an anointed queen of one country and soon would be of another. In the absence of the king, I should be obeyed, especially regarding my own son. My hands, resting on the sides of the chair, trembled slightly, from a mixture of fearful anticipation and excitement. Outside the castle an army waited to enforce my wishes. Never before had I felt so important, so able to control the outcome of events. To steady my hands, I gripped the arms of the chair, for it wouldn't do for the arriving lords to see me so unsettled.

After what felt an almost unbearable delay, but was likely no more than a few minutes, loud masculine voices were heard in the adjacent Outer Hall, and then Anna appeared, followed by the lords. All five were dressed as though for battle, wearing breastplates and carrying helmets. There were swords at their belts, and from their defiant and angry expressions it was clear they were ready for conflict. I'd chosen them because each was at least unfriendly to the Earl of Mar, feelings that had now obviously been vastly increased by the prevention of their forces from further entering the castle.

Although they'd been grumbling upon entering, in my presence all became silent as they knelt before me, close enough for my advanced condition to be unmistakable. By now, I could barely contain the tension within me, and I gripped the arms of the chair so tightly I wondered if the wood would break. But in a steady voice, I told them to stand, and began the little speech I'd been practising for several days. "Good friends, please accept my most heartfelt and sincere gratitude for such a speedy response to my appeal for assistance. When I made it, I wasn't yet sure I would require it. But circumstances have unfortunately played out to show my apprehensions were correct. The king has requested I arrive in England in time for the safe delivery of his new child, and to do so I must leave immediately. But I cannot without the prince at my side, which the wife and heir of the Earl of Mar now seek to prevent. It is to overcome that obstacle that I have called you here. I now hope you can help me to accomplish my aim, and earn yourselves the eternal gratitude of your queen, and the prince, and, when the full matter is made known to him, your king."

"Good King James," one of the men loudly muttered. "A disgrace, that his family should be treated so by this dog of Mar."

At the door Lord Erskine appeared, at the head of a number of guards. His insecurity was plainly visible and before he could speak, the lords strode over to him. "What's this about not giving the prince to his mother?" one nearly shouted. "This is your queen!"

"By order of the king, we are charged not to turn the prince over to anyone." The young man was struggling to maintain his composure in the face of such formidable foes, all enemies to his absent father. I felt some sympathy for him, but it quickly dissolved when he added, "Even the queen."

Even the queen. Had James given them orders especially directed at me? It was startling to hear, stated so directly. The shock of it registered in my entire body, as though I'd been physically struck. The child, agitated, began to kick and move.

"Treason!" shouted one of the lords.

"It is you who are traitors!" Lord Erskine angrily answered. "I am loyal to our king, and Scotland! How dare you enter the residence of the prince with intent to disrupt it!"

"How dare *you* refuse the request of a queen!" another shouted back. "The king will have your head, and your father's, when he hears of it!"

"It will be your heads, my lords, chopped by the headsman from your bodies!" Lord Erskine's voice was shrill. "You come here on the pretext of assisting the queen, when your goal — all of you — is the throwing down of the earl my father! You are jealous of him and the favour the king has shown to the Erskines, and you take advantage of his being out of this realm in England! I tell you, the king has told us in no unclear terms that we are never to release the prince to the queen! She is not strong enough to maintain her own interests, and that of her son, among the likes of all of you! Our king is wise, and knows this!" He stepped back, but placed his hand on the hilt of his sword, as though ready to draw it. "It would serve you right if I had our guards cut you all down here where you stand! The disgrace of disturbing my father's house!"

"It is not your father's house!" a lord shouted. "Stirling Castle belongs to the king! You reside here in his service only."

The arguing continued, full of anger and threats, but apart from me, as though I weren't even present. I could scarcely believe the young lord had not only repeated that their orders were directly from James, but had underscored it by adding that I was woefully incapable of defending my own affairs. The thought that all in the kingdom might regard me as so unimportant, no more than an ornament to sit on a throne beside the king, was intolerable. Gripping the sides of my chair, I called out, "I am the mother of your prince!"

The arguing stopped and all turned to look at me. I rose to my feet, slowly, because the child was even more agitated, aware not only of my own feelings but seemingly sensing the turmoil in the room. Grandly, I said, "Lord Erskine, you forget you would not have any prince to protect were it not for me, who gave birth to him."

He replied, less stridently than he'd spoken to the lords but still without the slightest hint of apology or deference, "Madam, the king has said you are not to have him unless so instructed by himself. He has given us no such instructions."

"You need have no fear of disobedience. I know the king's mind in this matter and take full responsibility." I waved one of my hands at the lords. "These good gentlemen will confirm I have done so."

The lords instantly voiced their approval, although roughly and aggressively, showing they wouldn't mind continuing the contention. Inside me, the child moved suddenly, more strenuously than before, causing me to give a little gasp and touch my midsection. Seeing me do so, everyone became silent. Anna came up beside me and gently guided me back to my chair.

From behind Lord Erskine, the countess pushed her way through the guards just inside the door and stepped out in front of the lords. She came to me and curtsied. "Your Grace, last night I sent word to the council in Edinburgh by fast rider explaining your request and asking for their instructions. I have this morning sent another, describing —" she hesitated — "developments. Certainly, we'll receive a reply before sunset. These gentlemen can be shown to comfortable quarters until then, and of course be our honoured guests at dinner. May I suggest you retire until then as well? These unpleasant exertions cannot be good for you."

Beside me, Anna spoke out: "The queen needs to rest. This quarrel should not have been brought this close to her, in her condition."

"Tell your papist friend she speaks out of place here," Lord Erskine sneered defiantly.

There couldn't have been a worse place for me to learn that Anna's Catholic interests were known more widely than I'd thought, and were being used against me. Years of Scotland's religious struggles were now entangled in one which should have been only between James and myself. A feeling of utter futility presented itself as I saw how foolishly I'd underestimated the cost of coming to Stirling and taking Henry.

My despair must have shown somehow, if only to the countess, for her look of concern became even more pronounced, her sympathy for me as a mother superseding everything else. She wheeled about and faced them, and with bold authority said, "We await the instructions of the council. Now get out. All of you." Even from behind, her slender figure had gained a new stature. None of the men spoke, all remaining fixed where they'd stopped in the midst of their arguing, the conflict momentarily suspended, neither complying with the countess's orders, nor refuting them. "Go!" she ordered even more forcefully. To her stepson, she added, "You too, John, get these guards out of here. I charge you with treating these lords as our guests. The hospitality of the Earl of Mar will never be questioned."

There was the briefest of pauses, before the young lord said, "Gentlemen, please regard yourselves as our guests." Instantly, the tension in the room receded. The lords all bowed to me as they followed him out.

The countess turned back to me. "Let me help you back to your bed," she said gently. "This discord cannot be good for you, or the child." We were no longer a queen and a countess, but two women who'd borne children, and struggled to make their way in a world dominated by men. Our political differences had been rendered insignificant compared with our shared experience of childbirth.

Inside my bedroom, I felt better, and the child had become quiet again. I thanked the countess and told her I would rest until dinner. "Please let me know as soon as the messenger from Edinburgh arrives." But I knew that even with the fastest of riders, it wouldn't be until later in the day.

When she was gone, I said to Anna, "I must appear at dinner, before all of these lords. The countess managed them with great skill and authority. I must show I can at least do as much." I thought of the strength with which the much younger woman had faced them down. "Who'd have believed she had it in her? She was never like that before her marriage, when she was one of my gentlewomen at court."

"Marriage changes one," Anna said, implying it was why she had never chosen a husband. But her saying so was strange, because it had so clearly helped the countess better establish her position in life.

"It can bring things as well as take them away," I replied, then went on, "You were called a papist."

She made no reply. I hadn't expected her to, but I couldn't let it pass without comment. It wasn't the right time for a fuller discussion, which would come later. I then warned her, "Do not speak again in that way. It is dangerous, not only for you, but much more so for me."

I rested, and even slept a little. Shortly before midday I got up to prepare for my appearance at dinner. The child was now completely still, the poor thing likely as exhausted from the tensions of the morning as I had been. "No news from Edinburgh?" I asked Anna.

"Nothing yet. And everything here has remained quiet — which it should until we receive word from the council. Have you considered how you will respond when it comes, whether favourable to our cause or not?"

"It should be favourable. The council is equally divided between those friendly to the earl, and his enemies. But nearly all have at times sought to ingratiate themselves with me. Their attitudes to the lords I've called here vary, but if it's a choice between me and the Earl of Mar, they are going to choose whoever they expect to have the stronger voice with James, afterward." I stopped, troubled by my not knowing the answer to that already. But I was still the mother of a prince. I would see to it that everyone in Scotland and England knew that my voice with my son was strong, perhaps even stronger than his father's. And that prince, they all knew, would one day be their king.

"If the council's response isn't good," I said determinedly, "then we stay here at Stirling until I hear from James directly. We wait. I know he wants the new child to be English, and I must leave soon for that to happen. If James doesn't agree to allow me to take Henry, I'm going to make it clear to him I intend to remain here until he does."

The look in Anna's eyes told me that although she fully understood, she might not agree. Because of her Catholic sympathies, she'd encouraged me to take charge of Henry so as to avoid his appearance in England with a Calvinist guardian at his side, but she wouldn't go so far as to endorse my opposing the king. Yet I saw that even so, she wouldn't go against me. For emphasis, I repeated, "As I said, sometimes marriage can take things away from one."

As we approached the Great Hall, the sounds of many voices ahead of us told me the huge room was already full. I entered, and everyone stood, the lords all in places of honour at the front. But on the dais was only one setting for myself. The countess and her stepson were already present, waiting inside the door to conduct me to my seat, but Henry was nowhere to be seen.

Immediately, I was apprehensive; surely, they wouldn't have been so bold and foolish as to have removed him from the castle. "Where is my son?" I asked tensely, my displeasure clear in my voice.

Lord Erskine came to me and bowed stiffly. "We decided it best for him to dine in his apartments," he said officiously. "To shield him from any possible disruption."

I looked away from him, out into the crowded hall, where everyone was watching us. "Have him brought here at once," I commanded.

"No." There was unmistakable belligerence in his tone. Before us in the silent hall, someone gasped. Suddenly, an intense anger descended upon me. Struggling to hold it back, I was keenly aware that every eye in the hall was fixed on me.

He added, "We have been charged with the protection of the prince. Thus, we have made our decision." He folded his arms arrogantly.

It was a deliberate insult, in front of all the lords who'd come to support me. Any second it was likely they would object, something Lord Erskine had calculated. He had placed me in the position of now having to agree with Henry's absence, or bear responsibility for whatever brawl — or worse — might ensue, which would then absolutely confirm the correctness of their decision to keep him away. But if I meekly agreed, it would show me as irrelevant and incompetent, a queen that no one ever need pay attention to. No matter what I did, I couldn't win.

"Patience," whispered Anna behind me. But it was too late for such advice, and an angry torrent of words was forming in my head.

The countess, her face a perfectly controlled mask, took a step forward, and I felt a fleeting hope that she'd once again show her diplomatic ability. But before she could say a single word, I felt a sudden gush of wetness around my legs, followed by a nearly overwhelming cramping in my body, familiar signs of the onset of childbirth. The child was coming, but it was too early. Grief and fear immediately replaced anger and insult, and then a wave of pain rippled through me. I swooned backward as darkness descended around me.

Several hours later I was delivered of a stillborn boy. The birth had been exhausting, and more painful than any of my others, and I couldn't even summon the strength to speak as the hastily summoned doctors and midwives tried to elicit life from where it had departed even before a breath had been drawn. I stared blankly from the birthing chair as they wrapped the tiny body in linen and took it away. I felt only a numb vacancy, as though I were nothing more than the empty void where the child had been for so many months.

I tolerated being gently lifted and placed in the bed, and the further ministrations of the doctors, swallowing what medicines they put to my lips. But then being surrounded by an audience of doctors, midwives and gentlewomen, all looking at me sadly and speaking in hushed tones, became more than I could stand. "Get everyone out of here," I whispered. "Someone send word to the king that his child has been born dead. Make sure he knows it was a boy."

And as the heavy bed curtains were drawn around me and the late afternoon May sunlight was shut out, I pressed my face into the pillows and gave way to tears, tears I would allow no one to see or hear.

14

In the morning, despite still being weak and in pain and nearly overwhelmed by sadness, I knew I needed to recover as quickly as I could. Children of mine had died both before and after birth, teaching me that the grief of loss faded as time passed, and I knew there was no remedy for my current melancholy other than to tolerate it, and put my thoughts on current matters. With iron certainty I told myself the responsibility for the stillbirth rested with those who'd opposed me, including James, and I wouldn't hesitate to tell him so if he rebuked me. But the current unconcluded matter regarding Henry was urgent, and I plunged my thoughts into resolving it.

Anna looked surprised to find me already sitting up when the curtains were drawn back. After the accompanying doctors had attended to me, I waved everyone but Anna away. "How do things stand here now?" I asked. "What was the news from the council?"

"Perhaps it would be better not to trouble yourself with such matters until you are well," she hesitantly suggested.

"Attending to them is the best remedy for me. What news?"

"The council desires clarity of the king's intentions, which it is seeking. In the meantime, the lords were told to withdraw from the castle to the town below."

"That must have been before they knew of the loss of the child. I assume further messages were sent?"

"At once."

"Many are going to be wary of James's response to this. All should now take care of what they do next. As for myself, I am more resolved than ever not to set foot in England without Henry at my side." I then called for paper and pen to write to James. It was important he knew the child had been lost because of the opposition of the Earl of Mar's son. If that wasn't sufficient cause for James to finally separate himself from that entire family, I didn't know what would be. The loss of the child had been tragic, but some good might yet come of it if that could be accomplished. And in the meantime my anger at the earl would be a balm for grief, and fill the void within me.

What followed were a succession of days filled with tense uncertainty, with much coming and going at the castle by those of importance in the kingdom, council members and earls and other lords, and many letters arriving and being sent. The lords who'd come to my rescue had remained in the town, and visited me several times. News of what had occurred had spread, as well as the role of the earl's family in it, and unrest had been provoked throughout the land. In some places, I was told, there were even gatherings with the intent of preventing Henry from leaving Scotland at all.

The Earl of Mar returned, and I refused to see him. Anna reported, "He immediately drew his wife and son and staff together to hear their account of what had happened. They met in the chapel, of all places. Clearly, they are fearful of consequences. The earl then wrote a letter that was sent to England. Of course, it must be to the king." My own letter to him had been sent several days earlier, in which I'd pointed out Lord Erskine's papist remark and expressed my fears that the earl and other Calvinists were unfairly portraying me as one.

While the chaos swirled around me, I stayed in my bed and recovered my strength, and waited. I'd already had one letter from James, which he'd dashed off immediately upon hearing the news of the miscarriage, and it was loving and full of concern for my well-being. But the one that followed a number of days later, in reply to mine to him, was more meaningful. No one, he wrote, ever dared to criticise me to him, and the Earl of Mar had never suggested I was a papist. And then, finally, there was another letter, simple and direct: Henry should accompany me when I was well enough to travel, first to Edinburgh, and then to England. On our way to Edinburgh we were to stop at Linlithgow, where Elizabeth would join us. The three of us together would then cross into England at Berwick, where leading English noblewomen would greet us and bring us south.

When I finished reading the final letter, I folded it, and then held it between both my hands, reluctant to release it, the message in it having been so hard won. It was almost impossible to believe that, after so many years, Henry was finally to be placed in my care. The victory had come at a great price, one that it had been impossible to avoid paying, and my resentment toward those who had demanded it ran deep. But it was time for me to leave the battlefield behind.

I called for my women and told them I would dress, and today be up and about, for the first time since the miscarriage. It pleased them, especially Anna, who gave me one of her rare smiles, and they hurried away to select my clothes. Then I slid out of bed and walked barefoot to the window, and looked out over the castle grounds and spreading green landscape beyond. Once I left, I would never return here, even if I came back to Scotland again. But as I watched the soft white clouds drifting by, I was taken by the absolute certainty that in leaving Scotland, I would be leaving it for good. Something undefinable had been concluded over the past weeks, if not resolved.

An English noblewoman who'd arrived in Edinburgh several days earlier was waiting to see me when I arrived with the children back at Holyrood Palace. The Countess of Bedford had ridden ahead of the party that was to greet me at Berwick, to pay her respects. It was an obvious attempt to ingratiate herself, and I wondered if she wanted something specific. At the same time, it was commendable she had so exerted herself to be the first to greet and honour me. Although I was tired from the long coach ride, I had her sent up to my audience room, where I sat to receive her with Henry and Elizabeth on either side of me, resting their heads on my shoulders. I'd fought hard to be able to initially impress the English the way I wanted to, and this intrepid countess would be the first. "No doubt she'll be haughty and full of pride and expectation that I should be flattered she went to such trouble to be the first to see me," I told the children. "We must all try not to laugh at her arrogance."

But the young creature who entered, striding across the room to us as though in a hurry while her own attendants hovered by the door, was nothing of the sort. She was in her early twenties, and youthful despite a face that showed she already knew too much of disappointment. Reaching me, she knelt down and nearly touched her head to the floor. "I am your humble servant, madam," she said plainly, as I stared down at her perfectly coiffured thick brown hair. "I have come here to assist you in whatever way I can in the journey ahead of you. Last month, my father Sir Harrington had the honour of entertaining the king on his way to London. My own home is too remote for that, but perhaps I can be of service in other ways."

There was a sincerity in her voice that was touching, even though her refined inflections indicated much formal education. I told her to stand up, and I saw her face again — heart-shaped and small-featured, not really pretty, but with intelligence visible, especially in her frank and alert dark eyes. If I asked why she'd come, she would likely reply honestly: she was there to seek my favour, but also to befriend me. She'd calculated — correctly — that I would find having an English friend at my side of enormous benefit when I entered England, to help me fit in. There was going to be a maze of English details and differences I would need to be guided through. I'd already noticed her English was accented differently to mine, and that her lace-trimmed dark red satin dress with brocaded sleeves was in a somewhat different style to mine.

I called for Anna to take Henry and Elizabeth to their rooms. "The prince and princess," I said to my visitor. "I'd have you speak with them, but they are tired."

Her gaze followed as Anna led them away, then lingered on the closed door they'd departed through. She said, "None of my children survived infancy." There'd been the tiniest quiver in her voice as she'd said it. Turning to me, she added, "I am sorry for your recent loss."

"I've lost others before," I said haltingly.

"It feels unendurable. I know." A very small sigh escaped from her lips. "But one endures. And overcomes."

Yes, she did know. All at once, I was crying. "A boy," I said through my tears. "I saw him before they took him away. A beautiful boy. But he never breathed."

She knew enough not to offer soothing condolences, but instead simply stood, waiting. When my tears had stopped, she said, "My name is Lucy, madam. Lucy Russell."

And I saw that she had also come because she was lonely, and searching for a place in life, and thought that a new queen with a family might be it. With sudden insight, I saw that my years in Scotland had also been very lonely ones, political necessity keeping others at a distance. But in England, things could be different.

"Send for your things," I told her. "I'd like you to stay with me here in the palace until we leave for Berwick, in two days. There is much I need to know before I arrive there."

Later, she dined with me alone, and told me the plans for my reception. "The Earls of Sussex and Lincoln have been sent by the Privy Council to receive you. Both are in their early thirties, polished and sophisticated and charming, as well as handsome. Neither's wife accompanies them, but for very different reasons; Sussex's marriage is unfortunate, and they are separated, while Lincoln's wife is recovering from the birth of their tenth child. And so it is with the marriages of the entire English peerage: half are happy, half are not."

Half happy, half not. I drank from my cup of honeyed wine, tasting both its bitterness and sweetness. Half happy, half not would describe my own marriage. From Stirling I had written to James that I feared he did not love me, and had married me only because I was the daughter of the King of Denmark. In his reply he'd insisted that he did, and thanked God for it, because he should since I was his wife and the mother of his children, and not because of my royal birth. Had I been a cook's daughter, he'd written, once his wife, he'd have loved me.

"Life, I think, is half happy, half not," I said, appraisingly. James's letter had been reassuring. But I wondered if it was enough and how it would be for us in the years ahead, now that our mutual goal of the English throne was in hand.

I finished the wine and placed the cup on the table. A further goal had been the founding of a Stuart dynasty, and James hoped peace in Europe could be helped through international marriage alliances of his offspring. I stared at the empty cup. His attempts to balance the religious friction and discord in Scotland may have succeeded politically, but not so much within his own family, and in many ways, it had been responsible for the loss of the expected child. During that conflict, much had gone unstated, but Lord Erskine's remarks about Anna being a papist had been telling. But the Anglican clergy was less strident than the Calvinist, and it was possible in England those tensions wouldn't be so sharp, and wouldn't so strongly influence matters with the children. Despite the miscarriage, I was still young enough to successfully bear more. Perhaps the future would hold greater satisfaction for me as a mother, than as a wife.

The countess continued, next describing who else was already waiting at Berwick: "The Countess of Worcester, the Countess of Kildare, Lady Harrington — my mother, Baroness Scrope, Baroness Rich and Lady Walsingham. The countesses, like my mother, are well respected throughout England. The others are younger, although still older than us. Unlike the earls, most have happy marriages, except Lady Rich, whose marriage has been unhappy for years. Everyone knows it, but ignores it, the way the queen — Queen Elizabeth, I mean — did. In her final years she showed less interest in her courtiers and their lives. Politics held her interest until the end, but after that, her passion seems to have been her attire."

Visons of costly and exotic garments in an array of colours and fabrics danced before me. "It's said she owned two thousand gowns."

"More," Lucy answered, knowingly. "Most are out of style now, although she never saw it. Everything was opulent and ornate and full of artifice. Her make-up and wigs were also blatantly contrived, intended to detract attention from how aged she was underneath. She was always covered in jewels, as though she needed to remind people of her great value to them, and the kingdom. By the end it was all a little bizarre, although I can't deny that somehow it was impressive. But the court is ready for something fresh and new, and everyone in England is eager to see how you choose to style yourself. We've heard you have an elegance of your own."

"So, the English have expectations of me to set the fashion for the court."

"Yes, and with a wider view of society than the last queen's." Delicately, she added, "It's also understood that the king has little interest in such matters. His indifference to his own garments has already been noticed. His scholarship is well known, and there are already many who plan to seek his patronage. But for the arts, the intention is to look to you. And nothing is as noticeable as your attire."

"I've worn much white and red. I'll continue that for state occasions, but otherwise introduce more pastels. I've always tried to show authority in my dress, to impress that I was a queen equal to any. But things are different now. It might be better to remind the English that I'm young."

"A simpler style than Elizabeth's would suit you well. Something less extravagant."

"Pastel colours," I repeated. "Shades and hues that are paler than I've previously favoured. And instead of numerous necklaces and brooches, many ribbons and rosettes. Jewels are noticed more if they don't detract from each other. Although I must admit I am extremely fond of all kinds of jewellery, and fine garments. I love the beauty of them."

Lucy replied thoughtfully, "That can serve you well in England. Your use of them can make a point about your position as queen, and the importance of your family. For the last queen, people began to see her penchant for jewellery and garments as a replacement for the love that was absent in her life."

Unexpectedly I felt awkward, her comment troubling in a way I didn't understand. I looked away from her, down at the empty cup on the table.

She went on, "But the love between you and the king is known by all."

After the miscarriage, James had written that he'd loved me because he had a responsibility as my husband to do so. I'd told myself the response was enough — but was it? I said, "I've invited Mr Heriot, a wonderful maker of jewellery and trinkets, to come to London with us. I rely on him not only for myself but for gifts to others."

"We have fine craftsmen in England also, which you are soon to see. You're to be presented with gifts along the way to London. Several silver cups with gold angels have already been prepared for you and the children. The first is to be presented to you in York, where a great reception is planned. You can expect more at your coronation. And then, of course, many more at the New Year Celebration."

"I greatly look forward to the holidays. I miss the Christmas celebrations of my youth in Denmark."

"Christmas," Lucy answered, "is made much of in England. It's a public holiday, and one of the centrepieces of the court's activities. Queen Elizabeth enjoyed it greatly, and even the last one she celebrated was splendid. The entire palace is decorated with holly and ivy and winter greenery. Court is always well attended, with many entertainments and games, plays, music and dancing. Those courtiers with London mansions compete for royal attendance at their feasts and banquets. All types of sumptuous dishes are served, roasted swans or peacocks, and goose and wild boar, and Christmas pudding, and wonderful deserts of marzipan. Then, on New Year's Day is the gift-giving. The amount of gifts Queen Elizabeth received was overwhelming: jewels and garments and cups and vases and plates, and other fabulous and delightful objects. You and your family can expect no less, especially with it being your first Christmas as sovereigns. Everyone will be trying to impress you."

"Your advice is going to be needed for return gifts." Lucy's hand, delicate and white, with several rings on her slender fingers, was resting on the table, and I reached across and placed mine on it. "Lucy Russell, Countess of Bedford, I thank you for extending your friendship, which I accept with gratitude and reliance. I do not forget those who befriend me."

"Such is your reputation, madam."

I told her to go and rest; rooms in the palace for her and her attendants had been prepared. I'd already arranged for her to be present with my gentlewomen in the morning. Tomorrow, I'd again spend much time in conversation with her, learning what to expect in England.

She retired, and I remained at the table, thinking over everything she'd told me, and finally starting to allow myself to throw off the sadness of the miscarriage. But there was one thing yet to be done.

I stood up and called for my women. Anna came, but for once I didn't want her company for what I had to do. I sent the others to wait in the adjoining room, then said to her, "I won't have you with me for this. You try not to show it, but I know you cannot approve. Catholics don't recognise the salvation of children who die before birth. They are sent, I am told, to some strange undefined place called limbo. For once, I find the Calvinist belief softer and gentler. How could this child who never breathed not be with God in heaven? Perhaps if you were a mother you'd understand. But you are not, and you do not. And life has not yet taught you that sometimes religious beliefs can be wrong. All sometimes are, and sometimes right. But I cannot tolerate your disapproving presence beside me as we lay the remains of this last infant in the vault with his siblings."

Anna's face remained without expression. We'd already argued over it before leaving Stirling Castle, when she'd told me of ugly rumours that I was keeping the tiny coffin to show those who disbelieved I'd been with child, and had fabricated a pretence to diminish the power of the Earl of Mar. Her intention had been good, but she'd been trying to influence my actions in terms of her own religion in ways I did not appreciate. It wasn't the first time she'd done so, and her religion was drawing her further and further away from me. Perhaps the time had come for me to rely on her less, and seek the friendship of others. The arrival of the Countess of Bedford may have been timely for several reasons.

Anna silently retreated from the room, and when I went out to join the others, she was gone. "I'm ready," I told them, and we went out into the corridor, where two footmen stood with the small coffin. One of the palace stewards was there, with a great ring of keys, including that for the royal vault in the church. I went to the coffin and lightly rested my fingers on top of it, and once again felt loss and emptiness. But my tears were finished, and it was time to place the remains of the child who had almost lived in the vault. I stepped back, the footmen lifted up the coffin, and we began to make our way through the long, dark halls to the abbey.

Afterward, when it was done and I was back in my rooms preparing for bed, I felt the completion I'd hoped for. It was time to put sadness behind me, and look ahead to England, and to our new life. The satisfaction and exultant achievement I felt at now having Henry beside me as I entered England had been equalled in my life only by Henry's birth. My decision to have him there had been the right one, and the battle I'd fought to do so, worth it.

15

My certainty continued until we arrived at where James had arranged to meet us in England. All at once, grief for the miscarried child, which I'd thought had been left behind in Scotland, suddenly came over me as our coach made its way down the estate's long drive to the house. The sight of James in the distance, waiting at the front entrance flanked by noblemen and courtiers — ones I recognised from Scotland on one side, and new English ones on the other — was strange and remote, and he seemed unreachable.

As the coach pulled up and stopped, even the familiar faces from Scotland appeared as formidable as their English counterparts, and the rich and brilliantly coloured garments everyone wore, outshining those of the grandest of courts that had ever assembled in Scotland, were intimidating. Yet for all the splendour of the fine silks, velvets, brocaded clothing and feathered hats, the faces of all bore formal expressions of complete blankness. But the practised emptiness spoke volumes of the depths of feelings behind the masks, and was terrifying in a way that even overt hostility wouldn't have been.

A footman swooped over and opened the carriage door, and I saw an English nobleman coming forward to assist me out and lead me to James, visible several feet away. In his face I now recognised the features I knew so well beneath his tall and jewelled hat, especially the half-closed eyes. Love stirred in me, but caused more grief over the miscarriage as for the first time I acknowledged that the loss for him had to have equalled my own.

The nobleman removed his wide hat and said, "Welcome to England, Your Majesty. May I have the honour of presenting you to the king?" He extended a gloved hand to assist me.

On his face I saw nothing but the same blank look I'd seen on all the others outside. His voice, too, although striving for grandness, had sounded thin and empty. *Presenting me to the king?* It sounded as though he were introducing me to a stranger. I looked past his shoulder at James, and with dismay saw that pervasive formal emptiness on his face as well, rendering foreign the features which a moment ago I'd felt I'd recognised.

The gloved hand poised before me seemed ready to grasp me and yank me from the coach, and I shrank back from it, a small sob of fear escaping my lips. Then, Henry, seated across from me, sprang forward, forcing the English nobleman out of the way. Half out, Henry turned back to me and extended his own hand. "My lady mother, allow me to help you."

Encouraged, I grasped his hand and stepped from the coach. From somewhere, a voice rang out, proclaiming my name, and Henry's, and our various titles, and ahead of me I saw everyone bowing. I clutched Henry's hand, strengthened by it, feeling equal to whatever lay ahead. The voice rang out again, announcing Elizabeth, and I heard the swish of her gown as she stepped out behind us. Her presence too was reassuring, as well as the quick, brief thought of Charles, back in Scotland. So long as I had my children, I knew who I was, and would be, no matter how changed James may have been by becoming King of England.

And then, there he was, directly in front of me, and as we stood facing each other, there was mutual recognition, as there was in the embrace that followed. As I stepped back from him and gave way to tears, I saw an almost imperceptible grief pass across his face. It was the reassurance I had sought. My tears increased, this time not from dread, but relief.

James's face showed concern. Henry immediately said, "My lord father, the coach ride was long and difficult. So crowded were the roads the delays were constant, and my lady mother is exhausted. She needs to rest."

Behind me the long line of accompanying coaches of the nobility who'd met me at Berwick had pulled up. The Countess of Bedford appeared beside us, curtsied low to James, and asked, "May we conduct Her Majesty to the rooms that have been readied for her?" Even before he could answer she had taken my arm and was starting to take me past him.

"I intend to come to you presently, Anne," James said quietly. "It does my heart well to lay eyes on you."

As the countess and I stepped through the great door of the house, I looked back quickly to see Henry, handsome in his gold and green brocaded doublet, and green hose, silently standing next to James, while Elizabeth, charming in yellow satin and taffeta, was speaking to him in a lively manner, her hands gently fluttering. Henry had removed his flat velvet hat with its long white plume, and in the afternoon sunlight his fair hair gleamed as though golden, in a way that no crown could have made more regal. Elizabeth held herself with grace and dignity as she talked, but in a manner that in no way quieted her wit and exuberance. And before I turned away, I saw James smile broadly, in a way he almost never did.

"The king is proud of his children," I said to the countess.

"And of his queen," she answered. "You've made a splendid impression. The sincerity of your tears, and your feelings, was evident to all. I'm told the court has thus far found the king likeable, but a bit remote. But in an instant, your arrival, with your children, has changed all of that. You've provided depth to his regal demeanour. This is new, for these English lords about him here. Remember, the last queen in her final years appeared nothing more than a bejewelled but hollow figure of authority, isolated and alone. Now, there is a royal family that breathes and lives."

Something within me relaxed. The constant and endless socialising of our journey through England, at a sometimes frenzied pace, had rushed along as if part of some galloping dream. Emerging from it felt different, as though I were finally able to notice what surrounded me. For the first time, it seemed I was in a different country, a much richer one, the mansion I was walking through luxurious in a way none were in Scotland. The room I was shown to was richly panelled and had a high ribbed ceiling, the walls hung with tapestries to rival those in my rooms at Stirling Castle. There was a large canopied bed with blue damask curtains and covers, and all types of intricately carved oak furniture, tables and cupboards, and chairs and footstools covered with colourful velvet cushions. All around were delightful little pillows delicately embroidered with an array of flowers, fruit, birds and animals. Bay windows were open to allow in the sweet-smelling breeze from the gardens.

Footmen followed us in, bearing my trunks, which Anna directed to be placed and opened in various ways. The countess stayed, and with the other gentlewomen, helped me remove my hat and jewels, and white- and gold-trimmed travelling outfit, and change into a long silk robe and comfortable slippers. Lying down on the bed, the pillows and damask covers felt impossibly soft, their light blue colours like gentle water washing around me. "Why haven't we such fine bedding in Scotland?" I asked hazily, and heard my women laugh softly in response. As I drifted into sleep, it was with the thought that I had finally arrived in England, and been welcomed as queen.

Sometime later I awoke, feeling refreshed and as though I'd been asleep for days. But Anna, beside the bed, told me it had only been for an hour. "The king has sent word he is on his way. Shall we reply that you need time to dress?"

I sat up and ran a hand through my hair, which spread across my shoulders without any ribbons or clips. I pulled a lock forward and felt its softness, and saw its blonde colour, without the slightest touch of grey. I was not yet thirty, and still had my beauty. "No, my husband can see me without artifice. Let me remind him I am not only his queen, but his wife." Today, the lords awaiting my arrival, and their dress and manner, had been my first taste of how formal everything was likely to be in our new English lives. The party that had greeted me at Berwick had been festive, and merry and light-hearted — not an accurate indication of what was to follow. Today the Countess of Bedford had assured me I had lived up to expectations, and that James had been pleased. But I needed him to recognise and respond to me as we were beneath those formalities. He had, after all, written that had I been a cook's daughter, he'd still have loved me.

When he came in, I sent everyone else out, and greeted him standing alone in my simple robe in the centre of the luxurious bedroom. It was a stark contrast to how we'd met each other outside, intently observed by the leading nobles of the land. This time, it was us alone, and I only hoped that his attitude would be the same that I'd felt outside. As the door closed behind him and he crossed the polished wood floor towards me, I all at once understood how very much I wanted it to be. My time alone in Scotland, and my wondering of how it would have been to be a queen regnant instead of a queen consort, had been but a fantasy.

He spoke first, before reaching me. "I have missed you greatly."

"No more than I you." Even a day ago I wouldn't have known my own mind enough to be able to say it, but now I could.

He was hatless, and without the jewellery and fine cloak he'd worn outside. As he drew closer, I saw his grooming was more meticulous, his hair and beard more neatly trimmed than usual, and his garments fit perfectly; he looked more compact and less rangy. His gait was smoother, slower and more balanced, barely awkward at all. England agreed with him, and had already worked changes upon his appearance — good ones. But they were subtle, and I saw that he was still the same man, with the same face, not only in features but in expression. And as he reached me and we embraced, I felt it as well.

He stepped back but continued to hold my hand in his, as though reluctant to release it, and I made no move to let go. With his other hand, he touched my hair, running his fingers through it. "When I think of you," he said, "when I call up your image before me, always this soft cloud comes to mind. And then, the blue of your eyes and the smooth, cool whiteness of your face."

He reached into his doublet and withdrew a brooch, made of rubies and diamonds set in gold. "A small token of welcome. I hope you find it matches the quality of anything Mr Heriot has been able to provide us with. Accept it as a sign of the bounty that awaits you here in England."

I took it and saw it was indeed a beautiful thing, intricately made in the shape of a ship, likely intended to show the commencement of our English journey. "It's lovely, and unexpected. But you must wait to see me wear it. The silk of this robe won't support it."

His eyes, half closed as always, continued to observe me closely; he was as observant of how I would receive him, as I was of him. But if he'd been worried, he no longer was, and his lips formed a half smile as he replied, "Later then, when you're in queenly attire." His head tilted, and he leaned in as he asked, "You received the wardrobe of Queen Elizabeth? And her jewels, and other personal items? I had a vast quantity of wagons full of them sent on to you."

Waiting for me at Berwick had been trunk upon trunk of the old queen's fantastic gowns, transported at great cost and effort. The scope and richness of them had been legendary, and what I'd found had lived up to that reputation as the trunks had been opened and the contents taken out and viewed, filling an entire hall in the castle where we'd stayed. There had been gowns of velvet and satin and taffeta in every colour imaginable, brocaded and embroidered and trimmed with thread of silver and gold, and almost all bejewelled in some way. There'd also been separate sleeves, ruffs, gloves, girdles, hats, pomanders and fans. And then, in specially locked trunks, had been her jewels — earrings, bracelets, brooches, necklaces and tiaras. They bore diamonds, rubies, pearls and other stones I'd never seen before, all set in beautifully wrought gold and silver.

Although those first days in England had been dreamlike, distracted as I was by deeper concerns, that finery had made a vivid impression upon me. I had watched attentively as my Scottish gentlewomen had exclaimed in wonder over each new piece, while the English women enjoyed their awe in a gentle and good-natured way. But when all the trunks had been emptied and everything spread out in the cavernous stonewalled hall, there'd come a moment when everyone had been silent. The vast display of garments had seemed empty; they spoke of a woman whose life had been full of rich things but devoid of love.

But James had thought to please me, and the gesture had been touching. "Yes, they were in Berwick when I arrived. Thank you." There was no need to tell him I'd had them sent back to London. Dressmakers had already been consulted and new gowns, in my own style, had been ordered, and some already received.

A moment passed, during which from outside the open windows we could hear the sounds of the crowds that had followed us to the estate. The beautifully furnished room seemed an oasis of quiet and privacy away from the pressures of so constantly being the focus of attention, so much more so than we'd ever experienced in Scotland. James felt it also, and knew as I did that the time was right for things between us to be addressed.

He said, "I am sorry for your recent illness. And for the loss of the child. It was a great disappointment, but even so I am most grateful for your recovery." He paused. "And I'm sorry I was so far from you during your ordeal. I intend for us never to be so separated again."

My fingers closed around the brooch. At the entrance below he'd seemed proud of his children in a way I'd never seen him display before. How much prouder would he have been to have his assumption of the English throne graced with the immediate birth of a third son? It had been a unique moment, the perfect timing of which would never again be presented. And it had been lost.

Although I'd resolved to be moderate in my anger towards the Earl of Mar and his family, the sense of loss was more than

I could bear. "Hateful Earl of Mar!" I exclaimed, the hand holding the gift tightening into a fist. "How much more impressive would our reception in this country have been with the birth of a new prince? It is the earl and his family that have deprived you of that, as well as another son! Can't you see how this man causes discord between us? Surely now he can finally be removed from our lives before he inflicts further sadness upon us."

"Anne," he began. "I —"

But now that the words had begun, there was no stopping them. "And his horrible mother! She was a bitter and angry creature until the end. Even her final words to Henry, on her deathbed, caused him great distress. She said she was sorry for what his life would be."

James flinched and turned his head slightly to one side, as though he'd been struck, which surprised me, for he was seldom so natural, and every move of his was calculated and measured. The remark had troubled him.

"She was old," he then offered, but with little effort, as though saying so was futile. "And people's minds can wander at the end." But I saw that what I'd said had impacted him deeply in a way I hadn't expected. The moment was right for me to tell him as much as I could.

I continued, "It was inexplicable, and confused him. My arrival so shortly afterward was good in that I worked to lessen the bleak impression it had made upon him, despite the miscarriage, which I made every effort to distance him from even though he was right there in the castle when it happened. I wanted to distance him not from the disappointment, which we all must learn to accept in our lives, but from the anger, and the bitterness of the surrounding struggle. The change which then followed was good for him. It is important now for him to be removed from the company of those with such strong Calvinist beliefs. England is a different place to Scotland. I felt before that it would have been a mistake for you to have Henry presented here in the company of the Earl of Mar, and after seeing my reception in this country, especially here today, I feel it even more. The English lords surrounding you outside, despite their formality, were so full of life! For Henry to have appeared here at the side of the earl would have been out of place. I did the right thing, James, in preventing it."

He looked back at me oddly, and I saw that a new thought had occurred to him. He then said quietly, "I never intended for Henry to be brought here so. For the very reasons you now state."

He never intended for the earl to bring Henry to England? I stared at him, not understanding. "Then why had you sent the earl back to Scotland?"

"For stability — especially after your departure. But it was never my intention for Henry to arrive here other than at your side, and with our daughter."

What he was telling me was so startling I was at first unable to find any reply. Finally, I asked, "Then why had you not sent word of that? Why had you not told me, James?"

"I thought you already knew." He said it simply, but with resolution. Then he exhaled sharply. "I am sorry you believed I would have had it otherwise. I see now I was at fault for not having been clearer. My responsibilities here were a distraction. But many of them have now been settled, and they are not going to be so again."

So, it had been a misunderstanding, with the most sadly profound of outcomes. But my anger was still strong. We'd been deprived of another son, and Scotland had briefly been plunged into political turmoil. Forcefully, I said, "The Earl of

Mar must be reprimanded! It was the behaviour of his son that so troubled me as to cause me to miscarry."

Steadily, James replied, "Anne, you must put your anger away, and instead be thankful we have survived the crisis. It is important you do this, so as not to create discord here in England at the outset of our reign. What you say about the message that Henry's arrival in the company of so severe a Calvinist would have conveyed is correct. But you must understand all the same that for me to show disfavour to him would now convey the opposite message, which we must equally avoid. So even if you cannot move beyond your private anger, it is essential that you do so publicly."

I looked away from him, for it was difficult for me to say what I now needed to. "Don't think I fail to understand how my own feelings became a cause for politics. I've considered this much in the past month. I know this cannot be, in England. We must think of our children."

"I repeat, I am sorry for what happened. And I agree that the Earl of Mar isn't needed any longer as Henry's guardian. I've decided he is to have his own household now, and has no need of a guardian other than myself, and his tutors and staff. England should appeal to him. His desire for adventure should find many places for expression here, much more so than he'd ever have found in Scotland. The wealth here to support such endeavours is great. Already I've been approached by merchants urging the settling of the new lands across the ocean, the reports of the bounty of which are beyond imagining. Henry's education must continue with the aim of his one day ruling over such enterprises." He paused. "There is never going to be a need for anyone to apologise to him for having been born a prince. His opportunities here are great. But to use them effectively he must learn to be mindful of his position, and respectful, and his continuing education must include this. Also, you and I must demonstrate this in our own choices and actions."

Nothing could have made me happier than what James had said so far, erasing my concerns about his lack of awareness or understanding of Henry. What was now before him in England was exactly what I would have chosen for him. But the way James now folded his hands together caused me to think there was something else he was about to say to which my response might be different.

He said, "All three of our children must learn this. To those whom God has given more, more is expected. Our personal desires must always be secondary to the good of the kingdom. Because of this, I am considering whether or not it would be best for Charles to remain in Scotland."

I felt as if I was standing on sand that was starting to wash away. My sense of victory and accord was eroding. I wanted nothing more than the harmony between us that the conversation had thus far led me to believe would be possible. But at the same time, I knew there was no other choice for me but to confront the matter head on. Charles was my son as well as Henry, and deserved nothing less than as strong a stand as I'd taken for him.

"No. Charles should join the rest of us here as soon as he is strong enough to safely make the trip."

"Please hear my reasoning, Anne, before you take an opposing position," James replied, a touch of inflexibility entering his voice. "Scotland feels remote and distant to me now, in a way I hadn't expected. If I feel this way, so must our subjects there, and that cannot be. Having a child of mine, a son, remain there could be an effective substitute for my presence."

"You considered that with Henry but decided otherwise," I said tensely.

"It is different with him. The English needed to be impressed with us as a family. But God has blessed us with two sons. Upon reflection, I have come to the conclusion that he also wants one to remain in Scotland. It can be of great benefit in ensuring peace between these two kingdoms."

Unexpectedly, I laughed, but stopped quickly, since for James to think I was mocking him would only make it worse. Then I said, "We must always be careful not to let our faith become self-serving. God has been good to us, but we must seek to do his bidding, and not the other way around."

James was so surprised that he took a step backward, as though I'd physically pushed him. But I reached out and grasped his hands, preventing him from retreating further. "You speak as a king, but you must decide as a father as well. What good can come of our children growing up in a strange and remote manner? They must have some understanding of the human lives of their subjects."

"Our personal desires must be secondary to the good of the kingdom," he repeated, but this time the resolve in his voice seemed to waver.

I at once continued, "But the kingdom isn't well served by this decision either! You feel distant from Scotland because you've been separated from us. This should now change, with us here. Even from London, the border is merely a day's ride away. I don't disagree with the need to keep the Scottish aware of us, but it can be done through visits and other means. You already are doing so; you said the Earl of Mar was sent back for stability. Eventually, when he is older, perhaps Charles could reside there permanently. But for now, he needs to be close to us, not only you and I, but his siblings also. Especially his brother, who is one day going to be his king. Accord and amity must be strong between them. The Old Testament is full of tales of disaster when brothers become hostile: Cain and Abel, Isaac and Ishmael, Jacob and Esau. Both should not only be in one country, but in the same household."

James stood hesitantly for a moment, staring off into the distance. Then he turned away and moved towards the window, but stopped before reaching it and sat down in the closest chair. "How beautifully appointed this room is," he said vaguely, looking around. "The beauty and wealth of this country is going to astound you, Anne." He gestured to the chair beside him. "Come and sit by me."

His sudden change of mood was surprising but welcome, and seemed to herald a favourable outcome. There was something different about him, and even now as he'd crossed the room his walk had been smooth. I felt a new serenity as I followed him and gracefully seated myself as he'd requested.

He said, "Your argument is convincing. Let it be as you wish. Charles can join us here as soon as he is strong enough for the journey. Meanwhile, I expect you to put behind you your anger toward the Earl of Mar. Or at least make a show of cordiality and civility, if not favour." He leaned back in the chair and smiled at me. "Now, let us simply enjoy being once again in each other's company. I have missed you, Anne."

We remained so, seated side by side on the comfortable chairs in the beautiful room, for more than an hour, chatting quietly about all sorts of trivial things. When he finally, and reluctantly, departed, I sat for a long while by myself. Then I had Anna sent in to me.

"He's changed," I told her. "But in a way that is good beyond what I could have hoped for. Some great underlying fear that was always within him seems to have vanished. One that was never noticeable, and only is now through its absence. The reason can't be anything other than the peaceable attainment of the English throne. But it's almost too good for me to believe. I can only hope it's permanent."

"The weeks ahead should tell," she answered. "And then the months and years."

I had more to say to her, and had called her in to do so. The decision to go to Stirling for Henry had been agitated by her Catholicism, and I saw now the extent to which my own fears and dislike of the Earl of Mar had been exacerbated by her beliefs. Had she encouraged moderation and restraint, the outcome might have been different. But as I looked at her, standing silently before me, it was impossible to blame her for having advised me as she thought right. The decision to go had, in the end, been mine. Yet for the first time I fully saw how apart from each other we'd grown. From now on, I would remember to keep my own mind regarding affairs of importance. If I sought advice from anyone, it would be from my husband.

"Your Grace?" she asked, as though knowing I'd planned to say more.

But I only smiled gently and waved her away. As I watched her go, I could only wonder if she was as content as she said she was, in her solitary world with only religion for comfort. Possibly so; the world was full of different types of men and women. But for me, it would never have been enough.

James came to me that night, and stayed a long while, sleeping peacefully beside me in the soft English bed. In the morning he left me only briefly, as we both dressed and readied ourselves for our departure for the next estate. We'd arrived where we were separately, both uncertain of how we would find each other, but we were leaving united. And, many hours later, as we rode up in front of the next magnificent mansion, the English were able to welcome not only a king and queen, but a royal family, and the cheers and applause of those crowding along the drive and on the lawns before the house were a sign that a new time had begun.

HISTORICAL NOTE

In England, Anne of Denmark found the perfect setting for applying her love of beauty and finery in important ways. She found satisfaction in becoming a patron of art, music, theatre and dance. The respect given the culture of the Jacobean court throughout Europe was mostly due to her efforts.

A NOTE TO THE READER

Dear Reader,

Thank you for reading *The Queen's Cousin*, the third in my series of novels about the Tudor succession. This one is set as the sixteenth century closes and the seventeenth begins and the question of the heir to the Tudor throne is settled. My choice of Queen Anne of Scotland, wife of Queen Elizabeth's cousin James, as narrator was for several reasons, but mostly because I felt she has in the past been treated by novelists and historians as a background figure, with her own ambitions, triumphs and failures largely if not entirely overlooked. A goal of this series has been to bring forward such stories, which are either little known or which I believe have been misinterpreted. Anne's varied and interesting responses to her many children, and how the dynamics of her marriage shifted accordingly, also seemed as though they would have relevance to modern readers, especially the custody battle between her and James over their first son, Henry. Much is factually well documented, particularly the struggle over Henry. Although I am a novelist, I always try to adhere to known facts. Where I did use creativity was in the development of all characters' motivations and emotional responses, as I do in all my novels, taking into account the beliefs and societal standards of the time.

Almost anyone with an interest in historical fiction has at one time or another encountered the story of Mary Queen of Scots. Another goal of mine for this novel was to present what I felt had to be the profound impact of her legacy on the son she had barely known and the daughter-in-law she had never met, and how that in turn affected them as parents. A central theme of this entire series has been how ambition instilled in individuals by or because of their parents, directly or otherwise, later finds expression through their attitudes toward their own children.

My original intention was for this novel to be longer, following the family into later years. But while working on it two distinct stories emerged, and I have chosen to write them separately. The sequel to *The Queen's Cousin*, *The Queen's Children*, also narrated by Anne, begins in England shortly after the first one ends, and tells the tale of what happens as the children grow older and marriages are sought for them and they begin to take their places in the world. *The Queen's Children* is to be published by Sapere Books later this year, and I hope you'll look for it.

Once again, thank you for reading *The Queen's Cousin*. If you liked it, I would be grateful if you would post a review on **Amazon** and **Goodreads**. And please keep an eye out for the other novels that are coming!

Thank you!
Raymond Wemmlinger

Sapere Books is an exciting new publisher of brilliant fiction and popular history.

To find out more about our latest releases and our monthly bargain books visit our website: **saperebooks.com**

Printed in Great Britain
by Amazon